JUDGMENT HAS FALEN

RECLAIMING HONOR BOOK 03

JUSTIN SLOAN
MICHAEL ANDERLE

COPYRIGHT

Judgment Has Fallen (this book) is a work of fiction.

All of the characters, organizations, and events portrayed in this novel are either products of the author's imagination or are used fictitiously. Sometimes both.

Copyright © 2017 Justin Sloan and Michael T. Anderle
Cover by Jeff Brown www.jeffbrowngraphics.com
Cover copyright © LMBPN Publishing

LMBPN Publishing supports the right to free expression and the value of copyright. The purpose of copyright is to encourage writers and artists to produce the creative works that enrich our culture.

The distribution of this book without permission is a theft of the author's intellectual property. If you would like permission to use material from the book (other than for review purposes), please contact info@kurtherianbooks.com. Thank you for your support of the author's rights.

LMBPN Publishing
PMB 196, 2540 South Maryland Pkwy
Las Vegas, NV 89109

First US edition, 2017
Version 1.01 Edition February 2017

The Kurtherian Gambit (and what happens within/characters/situations/worlds) are copyright © 2017 by Michael T. Anderle.

DEDICATION

From Justin
To Ugulay, Verona and Brendan Sloan

From Michael
To Family, Friends and
Those Who Love
To Read.
May We All Enjoy Grace
To Live The Life We Are
Called.

**Justice Is Calling
Reclaiming Honor Team**

Beta Editor / Readers
Dorene Johnson (US Navy (Ret) & DD)
Diane Velasquez (Chinchilla lady & DD)

JIT Beta Readers
Micky Cocker
Maria Stanley
Kimberly Boyer
John Findlay
Ginger Sparkman
Sherry Foster
Alex Wilson

If I missed anyone, please let me know!

Editors
Stephen Russell
**Thank you to the following Special Consultants
for Judgment Has Fallen**

**Jeff Morris - US Army - Asst Professor Cyber-Warfare, Nuclear
Munitions (Active)
W.W.D.E**

CHAPTER ONE

Restaurant in Old Manhattan

Valerie breathed deep to take in the scent of lilacs and spring drifting over from the indoor waterfall. Surely, such a place as this had never really existed in the outside world. Too much of the world was barren, too much of her life full of darkness and misery.

Sitting here, feeling the high life some had at their fingertips while others struggled to avoid starvation or to get a roof over their heads, she was reminded why she had to change all that.

Why she had taken a stand to see that justice had its day.

A small part of her mind reached into distant memories, a youth long gone, when a scent like this meant a visit to a cottage in a mountain. Memories of long days spent swimming in a lake and evenings wearing a flowing, flowery dress spinning as she danced with her mother.

But those days were barely memories at all. She would

reach for them in the dark hours of the night, hoping beyond hope. When she would wake up, she remembered the futility of trying to grasp a complete picture of what life had been like before she had become a vampire.

So she blinked the thoughts away, focusing instead on the meal before her, and this beautiful setting.

The restaurant had been set up to please the CEOs when they were in town, before Valerie had scared them off and then executed their attack dog, Commander Strake. Looking around to her left, she could certainly understand why they loved it here—the walls were set up to look like slick rocks interspersed with tropical flowers, while the ceiling was painted orange and purple to feel like a sunset.

"You haven't touched your food," Jackson mentioned as he pointed to her plate with his fork. He sat across from her with a half-eaten grilled lamb on his plate and a glass of amber ale in his other hand, watching as she took in the scene.

She smiled. "I'll taste it, but…" She glanced around at several other couples eating, noticing more than one set of eyes darting her way as she leaned toward him just a bit. "Is all this extravagance necessary?"

"Is this what you wanted?" he asked. "Has it, what, fed the flames, as you put it?"

She nodded, but her mind was on the nearest couple, the ones between her and the door. As an old woman glanced over and smiled, a sensation swept over Valerie--one that burned of hatred, even nearly made her shake, she felt it so strongly. And one word, *murderer*.

Jackson noticed the change in her expression, so she put on a mask of ease and cut into her steak. When she lifted the tender, overly red meat to her mouth and bit into it, she moaned. He was right, it was delicious. Almost enough to make her forget her problems.

Almost.

The thought of a hungry child pulled at her gut, telling her that what they had achieved so far simply wasn't enough. Too many people in this city were struggling to survive, and she could no longer stomach the situation.

It was time to make a change.

In the week since defeating Strake, all she could think about was how they could rebuild the city. How to get food to those in need, and roofs over the heads for the people. They needed medical supplies and so much more just to keep them alive.

And of course, they needed security in case the CEOs made a return.

So far, at least, there had been peace here in the city.

Speaking with the former Enforcers that were held in cells back at HQ, she gathered that most of the military work had been conducted by Commander Strake, though it was financed by the CEOs. That meant that, while they would be able to build up a force again, it would take them time.

So, Valerie had a little time to relax for the moment, but she wanted to build up the city as much as possible, and that included knowing where the city stood. Who were the elites of the city, and what allowed them to continue their existence as such? Had they been part of the CEOs' network? Were they still *part* of that network?

Jackson was watching her face devolve back to a worried expression, but she gave him her best attempt at a smile and took a sip of the beer. Compared to blood, a taste she'd grown to savor, it was like muddy water.

A sudden dizziness came over her, followed by what could only be described as a tingling that ran up her body as emotions swept over her and words and thoughts that she couldn't quite place were coming from her surroundings.

She shook her head and looked around the room, realizing that the thoughts were somehow coming from the other people there, though trying to understand them was like walking through a dense fog.

Jackson looked around, before turning back to her, "Something's bothering you?" he asked, and she wanted to say *yeah, no shit*, but instead she clutched his hand and grimaced, blocking out the strange sensation before letting go.

"Let's get out of here." She whispered, then stood and was glad to hear him stand up and follow her.. She could feel the eyes of many on her as they left, she was heading towards the elevator in the hallway.

Again the sensation hit her, like she could feel annoyance coming from one place, hatred from another, confusion from the majority. Was this what Akio meant by reading minds, or would it become clearer as she became accustomed to it?

"You don't look well," Jackson murmured close to her ear.

Her head was spinning. Why couldn't they just get out of there? What was taking so long?

He wrapped an arm around her waist and pressed the button at the elevator.

When the doors dinged open, she nearly collapsed. Luckily, he had her. His muscles tensed as he pulled her close.

"What exactly is going on?" He asked, but then he released her, stepping back, face pale in shock. Shrieks sounded from inside the restaurant, and Valerie felt her energy returning, her mind clearing. The doors closed and they stood there, Jackson looking at her with terror and confusion.

She was doing it again, she realized. Breathing out, she focused on releasing any negativity stored in her mind, and was relieved to see Jackson's color return.

He stood, wobbly on his feet, and pressed "L" on the elevator panel, to head down to the lobby.

"Well, damn." He shook his head again, glanced her way, and then looked down at his pants. "At least I didn't piss myself, or worse," he said as he pretended to wipe down his legs.

She laughed and covered her mouth. "I'm—I'm sorry. That's only happened once before, when I was fighting Strake."

"Pissing yourself, or that crazy fear thing that I can only assume was you?"

"Real funny. The fear."

"Judging by the shrieks we heard, I'm guessing this is some sort of fright power you can push out to those around you?"

With a shrug she said, looking around the elevator, "Your bet's as good as mine."

But it wasn't, not really. She knew that. As close as they'd become over the last week, going on dates and seeing the city, both the high life of it and the low, she hadn't told him about Michael, or about how the ancient vampire's blood had apparently given her extra energy.

And given her more than that, she thought with a glance down at her cleavage.

Before meeting Michael, she was pretty damn sure those things were only half the size—nothing to scoff at, but nothing so eye-grabbing either. Part of her wasn't sure she liked it, but the part that enjoyed Jackson's lustful accidental glances in that direction was pleased.

As for the ability to scare others, she had only ever seen that from Akio. Now she wondered where she ranked with these others. What powers did she have, exactly? A vampire that could walk in the sun, cause fear to strike at the people

JUDGMENT HAS FALLEN

in the vicinity and, apparently, sense their emotions or … thoughts perhaps?

That last one was still throwing her for a loop, so she decided to ignore it for now, or at least try.

"You know I'd never hurt you, right?" She took him by the hand and pulled him close, putting her body up against his. The thought of what he'd said hit her, and she too was glad that the fear hadn't caused him to piss his pants, considering the fact that she was so tightly pressed against them at the moment.

"Then how do you explain my sore back?" he asked with a wink. "I'm pretty sure that was you."

"I'm pretty sure that was you being stupid." She pinched his butt and smiled at the way he lurched forward and snuggled up even closer to her.

The elevator door dinged open and they heard someone clearing their throat. They turned to see an old lady and two teens waiting.

"Excuse us," Valerie said, separating herself from Jackson before squeezing past them.

One of the teens didn't move, so that her breast brushed against his arm. The little shit did it on purpose, she thought as she turned, considering whether she should teach him a lesson. Jackson had noticed, however, and shook his head.

"The city has bigger problems than a horny teen," he winked, bringing her sense of humor back as the door shut behind them.

"But that doesn't mean I won't knock him on his ass if I see him again. And don't try to stop me," she glared at Jackson.

"Me?" He scoffed. "I wouldn't dream of it."

He took her hand and moved to lead her away from

SLOAN AND ANDERLE

Enforcer HQ, the towering building with the blue stripe up its side.

"Date's not over," he said. "Just because you got all emotional or something."

"Watch it." She pulled him back, noticing someone watching behind a dumpster at the next street down. When they darted away, she was certain. "One of yours?"

He looked to see what she had noticed, but frowned to see nobody there.

"Can all this last?" she asked. "I mean, to me it all feels like it isn't real, you know?"

"You've just never been able to relax and enjoy a normal life." He glanced back at the alley, and then pulled her in a different direction than he'd originally intended, but still away from HQ. "In your mind, it's too good to be true."

There was a pause from Valerie before she replied, "With the CEOs still out there… it is."

He bit his lip. Nothing to say to that, apparently. She followed him around the corner and past Capital Square. They turned down a different road and came out on a street that she knew led to one of the subway entrances they'd hidden, a doorway to Cammie's old underground hideout.

"Don't tell me you're taking me underground." Valerie was about to crack a joke about having plenty of privacy back in her office, when she saw him glance behind them suspiciously.

A movement, and then she saw her, framed in one of the nearby windows—the teenage girl Valerie had met in battle, the one she had spared. The girl stood right at the edge of the window, just barely enough for them to see her but hopefully not enough for anyone else to catch sight of her. She lifted a hand and gestured with what looked like a four and then

JUDGMENT HAS FALLEN

drew a "Z" in the air, before ducking away.

"We got trouble," he admitted to her, his voice low so it wouldn't carry.

Valerie's voice came back, calm, allowing her body to relax, and prepare. "What kind of trouble?"

"The kind I'd rather we don't meet with violence… My people," his voice equal parts anguish and annoyance.

"Wait, what?" Now, Valerie's mind was going a hundred miles an hour to figure out the situation.

But he was already pulling her along, and she wasn't resisting. This time the wave of emotion came from him—pulsing, a mixture of cool with piercing heat. Confident, but worried?

Then she finally pieced it together. "So, they know what happened at Enforcer HQ, when you attacked. That my people were responsible for the deaths of many of yours."

He led her along a curving road with tall buildings on each side, then motioned to someone in a window watching, then another from the other side.

"Turn around." He put a hand on her back and they moved into the shadow of a doorway. "Just go back to HQ, I'll deal with them," he asked, his focus not on her anymore.

"You don't think I can handle myself?" She asked, her arms crossing in front of her chest, an eyebrow raised.

His lips pressed together, "I know you can, and that's what worries me." He glanced back up the street, to where three men and two women had appeared from a building and were approaching, cautiously. "I don't want more of my people hurt."

She nodded down the street, "Then come with me, at least. I don't want to see you hurt either."

He shook his head. "As much as they might be out for

blood, it won't be mine. There are still enough loyal to me that I don't have to worry... I hope."

The voice was cold, scratchy, "You eating with the devil again, Jackson?" one of the women called out, an older one with a thick, red coat. Even from here, Valerie could see the glimmer of sunshine as the woman spat on the ground.

"Go!" Jackson hissed, then pushed himself forward so that she was out of their line of site. "Allore, this isn't the time or the place," she heard him say as he walked towards them.

"You're walking a thin line here," the woman, Allore, replied. "Hand her over."

Valerie thought about staying and confronting this woman, but Jackson had a good point.

If they pulled out weapons and tried to attack, Valerie was likely to hurt them, or worse. That wasn't her intention or her desire. Well, it mostly wasn't her desire, so she quickly stepped over the stairwell, back into the narrow gap between apartment buildings, and made her way out of the alley.

She found a fire escape and did a push kick off of the brick wall to reach the first landing, and then pulled herself up before moving quickly up the steps to the top of the building. Soon she was clear, but doubled back to one of the nearby rooftops, where she knelt at the edge and peered over to view the scene stories below her.

If they were hurting Jackson in any way, she'd leap down without a second thought and end them all.

But they were talking and, it seemed, he was winning them over. They were still standing around with arms crossed, but none of them had hands on hidden guns, not that she could tell.

She sighed and turned back, sitting on the edge of the roof and watching the rays of light shooting down through

JUDGMENT HAS FALLEN

the billowing clouds. It was a beautiful sight, but one she realized she might have to see less and less of.

If she was going to enforce justice and keep this city in check, she was beginning to understand, being out in the open might not be for the best.

It was too divisive.

It was time Valerie returned to the shadows.

CHAPTER TWO

Post-Apocalyptic Attempt at a Dive Bar, Old Manhattan

Sandra was looking through the window, up at the sky and wondering if she'd really just seen Valerie running across a rooftop to then disappear over its side. No, she had to have imagined it.

Diego moved to the window beside her and gazed out. "What is it?" He shrugged and smiled back at her. "Looking to see shapes in the clouds?" He pointed, "That one looks kind of like a snake, right?"

"Huh?" She glanced back out and saw what he was talking about. Though, if you considered the sunlight at its tip, she could almost see it as something more humorous, and laughed.

Then he saw it too and rolled his eyes. "Let's stick with snake."

"Call them whatever you want," she said. "That one's pissing sunlight all over us."

JUDGMENT HAS FALLEN

"You know, you've gotten weirder lately." He made his move by sliding a little wooden play piece across the board and smiled. "Usually I like it."

"Just not when it involves clouds that look like man-parts?"

He laughed. "No, I guess even then, too. Your turn."

She looked down at the board before them. Diego had brought her here saying it was this great find, a dark bar high up in one of the few tall buildings remaining, where you could play vintage games like this one while sharing a beer. What had he called it? Chest, or something like that. With a shrug, she took a sip of her beer and cringed.

"That bad?" Diego asked.

She smiled, then moved one of the game pieces, still not exactly sure what she was doing.

"You didn't really listen when I explained how this game works, did you?" he asked.

"Sorry. I don't know." She bit her lip, feeling bad. She wanted to give him her full attention, she really did. "It's Valerie. I'm worried about her. Maybe it's nothing, but she's been off with Jackson so much this last week, I feel like I'm losing her."

"You do realize it's only been a week though?" Diego took a long swig of his beer, with only a slight shudder. "Not the best stuff in the world," he said, assessing it. "But considering they don't even have beer in most of the remaining world? I think I can handle it. And yes, Valerie will be fine."

"Maybe."

"Sandra, this is Valerie we're talking about here. Did you not see her in action? She's taken down a badass vampire, her brother no less, and Commander Strake. She saved half the vampires in this city from being drained of their blood so that the CEOs could stay youthful and rich, and as far as I'm concerned, she's a damn Goddess."

"Is that so?" Sandra frowned.

"Oh, not like that." He laughed and finished his beer. "Maybe that's the wrong word. What is it the stories used to talk about? There were those old ones you still hear people mention, about mutants who fought for those who couldn't fight for themselves. Superheroes, I think they called them? Yeah, that's Valerie. She's like a superhero."

Sandra nodded, getting what he was saying. Of course, she wished the rest of the city saw it that way. Reports came in often of the word on the street, and it seemed pretty split between half of the city seeing her as a liberator and, maybe, even potential leader, while the other half thought of her as a monster. Ella was out there spreading her rumors about Valerie, along with some of the vampires that had come with Donovan and possibly even some of Strake's Enforcers that had escaped the recent fights.

She glanced back at the beer, contemplating another sip. Did any of that matter right now, when she was supposed to be sitting here having a great time with Diego? She tried to tell herself no, that it didn't.

Maybe if she had something other than beer to take the edge off, it'd be a different story.

"You know what I'd love?" she asked, then pointed to the chess board. "Aside from kicking your butt at this game that I totally don't understand. Wine." She paused, pursed her lips, "Wine, and cheese, mostly."

Diego took a moment to see if he could think of any options but settled for saying, "Wine and cheese?"

"Oh, and a good bakery!" Her eyes lit up, but the moment was lost as her stomach rumbled.

JUDGMENT HAS FALLEN

"I told you we should've gone out to eat with Valerie and Jackson," he said. "You're hungry for more than bar nuts. Come on, let's go get you something good."

"If it's a bakery…"

"I haven't noticed any, but we can see what we can find."

He motioned to the bartender for the bill, and then chugged the rest of his beer, with a grimace.

She nudged him on his shoulder, "You don't like it either, admit it." She laughed. "See? If we had wine, like they have in France, maybe this city wouldn't be so glum."

"People in France are happier?" Diego gave her a doubtful look. "They've made barley whiskey in Spain, and that hasn't helped much."

"Good point." She frowned, then smiled again. "But imagine how much less happy they'd be without it, right?"

"Touché."

The memory of a glass of wine with Valerie brought back the sweet taste in her mouth that night when they'd sat on the rooftop. That night when Valerie had kissed her. She found herself blushing, but when Diego asked where her thoughts were, she stood, pushed her shoulders back, and said, "It's decided. Let's do it."

"Sure, great. But… what is it?" He looked at the board again, frowning, before looking up again. "And does this mean I win?"

She laughed and took the little piece that had a crown on top, then placed it on its side. "We both win. You at this silly game, me at life. Because I'm going to get the best bakery in the world going in this city, and I'm going to see to it that we have wine."

"We have bread," he said with a shrug. "Valerie told me about a place with these sausages served in bread."

SLOAN AND ANDERLE

"The man selling them calls them hotdogs," Sandra said with a dismissive laugh. "But if you call that bread, you've never had real bread. Come on."

She pulled him up by the hand to lead him out of the bar.

"What, we're doing this now?" he asked, slapping a few coins on the counter quickly. The heavyset man gave him a nod and blew smoke from a long pipe, leaving them with a sweet cherry scent on their way out.

"You ever found a better time to start something than now?" She threw back over her shoulder.

"Where would we even begin?" he asked, following her up the stairs to the roof, where they'd been able to park the police pod she'd piloted over. The wind was blowing strong up here, clouds passing by now, bringing with them a wall of gray in the distance.

She slid her palm across the door so that it clicked and then slid open, up and out of the way. "I'll figure it out. I always do, right?" A giggle escaped her as she slid into her seat.

Diego slid in on the other side of the vehicle, "Wow, you're worked up,"

"Hell yes I am." She looked at him, and then said, "You're right though. What's the rush?"

He looked at her with confusion, but when her hand was at his zipper and her lips pressed against his, she was pretty sure he got her meaning. It was like the excitement was boiling up in her. This wasn't about defending the city or fighting for their lives, it was about having fun and enjoying themselves. So a little rooftop foreplay wouldn't hurt in the meantime.

She undid his pants as he popped open her shirt, and then a voice sounded, "Sandra, it's—oh God, seriously?"

Retracting her hand Sandra spun to see that the display

showed Cammie's face, scrunched up like she'd just eaten a rotten apple.

A quick glance at where Sandra guessed the camera was gave her a pretty good guess as to why Cammie was making that face, so she placed a hand over Diego's crotch and said, "Might want to zip up."

"Thank you," Cammie said, glaring. "Not that I haven't seen it before, but—"

"Is there a reason you're calling?" Sandra interrupted, annoyed at the thought that Cammie and Diego had seen each other nude on more than one occasion. She got that it was all part of the way Weres operated—they generally would be naked when transforming, or tear their clothes and be mostly naked when they transformed back to their human forms.

That didn't mean she wasn't allowed a little jealousy.

"It's certainly not to catch you two about to tarnish a police pod's purity," Cammie said with a grin. "So… maybe find a hotel next time?"

"Laugh it up, bitch." Sandra playfully flipped her off. "At least I'm getting some."

Cammie laughed. "I could walk into any room here at Enforcer HQ and have ten cops, and another ten Weres or vamps tearing their clothes off with the snap of my fingers. Shit."

"Ladies?" Diego said, finally presentable again, aside from the deep red of his cheeks. "The point?"

"Ah, yes." Cammie's expression became serious again. "Valerie just got here and called a meeting. Seems she's got some big announcement and wants everyone in the room, pronto."

"Maybe… give us fifteen?" Sandra said, with a hopeful glance Diego's direction.

SLOAN AND ANDERLE

"Girl, do what you gotta do," Cammie said with a scoff. "You know Valerie better than I do, but if it were me, I wouldn't want to piss her off."

"Fine, see you ASAP." Sandra turned off the screen and then frowned at Diego.

"So…?" He looked at her hopeful.

"They don't actually turn blue, do they?" she asked as she started up the pod.

"Damn, that's cold. You're going to turn me down like that and mock me in the same sentence?"

"It's a genuine question." She swiped her fingers across the controls so that the pod's anti-gravity kicked in, and then glanced his way. "And think of it more as prolonging the pleasure. You know I'm good for it, and you know this girl's going to get hers," she quickly glanced down at his lap before looking out the front, "too."

He laughed and adjusted his pants. "I'll be fine, but if this meeting lasts longer than five minutes, I might fake a seizure to get us out of there."

"Deal," she said with a laugh, and then aimed the pod for the tall building half-way across town, with its blue stripe it was rather hard to miss.

For good or bad.

CHAPTER THREE

Enforcer HQ

Wallace entered the barracks floor, as they'd taken to calling the ninth floor of Enforcer HQ, where most of the cops, now Valerie's soldiers, had been set up with rooms. Some had families and returned home each night, but those who didn't were asked to stay here in case they were needed for defense.

He walked down the hallway and nodded to the cop on duty, seated behind a desk. The guard was the only one inside wearing his police cap, so you knew he was on duty. Although Valerie had taken to referring to them as her army, it was easier all around to still call them cops, or police officers, since that's the uniform they all wore. He was still hopeful she wouldn't change that—for him, the uniform was a grand tradition, and held certain levels of prestige.

"Any sign of her yet?" Wallace asked, glancing at the cop's name to remind himself. "Buland?"

SLOAN AND ANDERLE

Buland just shook his head. "They said you'd be by to ask, and that if you did, to watch my back."

"And why's that?" Wallace asked with a frown. He didn't consider himself harsh, or someone known for losing his temper.

"You never seem to like the answer, and now with your friends in power…."

He put up a hand, "Hey, I just want to make sure that if anyone hears anything about Ella, I'm the first to know." He folded his arms, very cognizant of the couple of heads that had poked out of doors. After a moment, he said, "So, nothing?"

"Nothing." Buland glared. "As I said."

"Right." He was about to go and leave it at that, but then paused and turned back to the man. "You do realize I'm in charge here?"

"If you have to say it, maybe it's not as true as you think."

"The hell's that supposed to mean?"

Buland raised an eyebrow, glancing behind him at the others who'd exited from their rooms and were standing by with curiosity. "We've been hearing things, right guys?"

The others shrugged while one shook his head but avoided Wallace's gaze.

"Now might be a good time to tell me these things," Wallace said.

"Come on, Wallace. You were a street cop, right?" Buland stood now, hand on his arc rod, as if Wallace might attack him for what he was saying. He had to admit, a part of him certainly wanted to. "A sergeant, right? And now you're suddenly in charge here, because *she* says so?"

He felt his cheeks flushing with anger. Where the hell had this talk been a week ago when everything was falling apart around them, when Strake's armies were invading, and when they were fighting the vampires and Nosferatu? They were cowering behind his leadership, that's where.

Wallace looked at the heads sticking out and then back to Buland, "Who's got a problem with it?" he asked.

"Top brass," Buland said. "I'm not saying I'm with you or against you," his chair squeaked as he changed his sitting position, "but let's be honest. We serve the uniform, which means we have no choice but to follow rank."

Wallace chewed on his lip a moment, "Given the cleanse that happened with the old Enforcers and the few corrupt cops that went with them, I'd say that only leaves Colonel Anderson." He glanced back at the other cops, thinking hard.

"I'm with you, if it comes to it," one of the cops said. Wallace recognized him as Karl Mason, one of the younger guys who'd started only a couple of weeks before everything fell apart with the arrival of Valerie, Sandra, and Diego.

Wallace nodded his thanks, but said, "Just make sure Major Donnoly is there beside him on that day, and we'll sort this out."

He gave Buland a judging glance before turning back and heading for the elevator. About halfway there, Karl caught up and said, "Sir?"

"No need for that," Wallace said.

"Right." The kid looked at him, nervously. "It's just… there have been rumors about her. The others have been told to keep their mouths shut, but I thought you should know."

Wallace stopped now, conscious of the others who were glancing their way but pretending not to. "What sort of rumors?"

"Threats mostly, of an underground movement that means to strike back at the city. Some are saying Ella plays a key role in the group."

Wallace felt his heart clenching. He wanted to believe this wasn't possible from her, but he'd been with her long enough to know that when she felt strongly about something, she went in with one-hundred percent.

It's how they had ended up together in the first place—when she'd seen him and decided they would be together. He had tried to protest, given that his partner was her brother, but she wasn't having it.

So they'd gotten together and soon he couldn't imagine life without her. He was sneaking off behind her brother's back so they could go on a date or sometimes a little more, and now it was like a part of him was simply…

Missing.

To think that she was possibly involved in an underground movement, maybe even an attack against the city, was gut-wrenching.

"Have you seen Peterson?" he asked, figuring that, if anyone could talk to her, it'd be her own brother.

The young cop shook his head.

"If you see him, send him my way," Wallace said, and then thanked Karl before continuing to the elevator.

While it hurt that his lover had run off on him like this, even switched sides, he knew that he wouldn't be able to handle it if his partner had done the same. The fact that nobody seemed to have seen him in a day or two made Wallace worry.

When the elevator doors opened, Colonel Anderson stepped out and gave him a look of disgust. His white hair was slicked back, his graying black mustache trimmed to perfection, and he stood a good foot taller than the next tallest man or woman on the force.

JUDGMENT HAS FALLEN

But none of that mattered to Wallace, because he wasn't in the mood to take shit from anyone.

"You have something to say to me?" Wallace challenged.

"Soon enough," the Colonel said.

Wallace glanced back to see Karl there among five others. Him and Karl against the rest, most likely. Not the best odds.

So he stepped into the elevator and turned to stare the Colonel directly in the eyes, letting him know his stance on the matter of leadership. When the elevator doors slid shut between them, Wallace breathed heavily through his nostrils and practically punched the number for Valerie's office.

This was not going to be fun.

When the elevator let him out, he stepped into the wide, open floor that had Valerie's desk at the far side along a wall of glass, and curved back behind him for a few offshoot rooms.

"Valerie?" he called out, but could tell by the silence that she wasn't there.

He walked over to the walls of glass and stared out at the city. It looked so peaceful, in spite of the wall of gray clouds moving in like a tsunami about to crush them all. Not the best of omens, that was for damn sure. Anyone on patrol tonight was certainly not going to have fun walking around in that storm.

Several police pods were approaching the building and moved around to the side and out of his line of sight, likely going to the floor that opened up as a pod bay. He turned to watch the last of them disappear from sight, then noticed the light on the elevator ding on.

A shot of panic went through him as he considered the possibility of the Colonel making his move like this, with Valerie out. But when the elevator doors opened and it was just Cammie, he sighed with relief.

SLOAN AND ANDERLE

"I wondered if anyone would be up here looking for her," Cammie called over to him and waved him her way. "Come on, Valerie has called everyone together and is waiting in the conference room."

"Finally got it cleaned up, did they?" he asked, remembering the way it had been shot to hell and covered in blood after the attempted meeting with the city's faction leaders.

"Let's hope so." She smirked and added as he joined her, "If not, you get the bloody chair. I can't go staining my only set of nice clothes."

He laughed, looking her up and down, eyes open in surprise. "What is that, stretchy pants and a robe?"

She twirled around for him, showing off her loose pants that came to a close around her ankles and the robe that she'd draped over her shoulders and tied around her waist. "It's the newest fashion, because I say so." She stopped and adjusted the shoulder cloth. "That, and it's super convenient for if I want to transform. Doesn't rip, though it might fall off, depending on how strenuous my following activity is."

"Nice," he said, nodding. "Shall we continue our little fashion discussion, or do you think this Valerie thing is possibly more important?"

"Maybe I just lock you up here and say you changed sides like your girlfriend?"

"Fuck you." He didn't mean it, and cringed as soon as the words left his lips. "Sorry, I just—"

Cammie held up a hand, her eyes flashing anger, but then she breathed deep and said, "No, my mistake. Not something to joke about yet, clearly."

He gave her a nod and walked over to the elevator with her. "Truce?"

"What, like no more crappy joking from me and you

don't talk down to me like I'm some piece of cat-turd you found on your shoe?"

He frowned, not sure how to respond to that, but she laughed and clapped him on the shoulder.

"You need to loosen up, my man."

"You have no idea." They stepped into the elevator together and he looked at her, completely serious and somber. "All kidding aside, do you have my back?"

"What?" She looked over and smiled, thinking this was the start of a joke apparently, but then saw he was serious and nodded, her smile dropping. "You know I do."

He pressed the elevator button and he said, "Good. It looks like former leadership among the police might make a move against me. I have a plan, but I need to know you and yours will be there in case it goes south."

"You can count on us, big guy," she said. "But if you say the big F-you to me ever again, you'll be eating your own asshole, got that?"

A chuckle escaped his lips before he saw the wild look in her eyes. "Yes ma'am."

CHAPTER FOUR

Enforcer HQ

Valerie paced the floor at the head of the conference room while the others waited silently. She wasn't sure how to best approach this, but she knew what had to be done.

Tiny droplets of rain were beginning to pelt the window—now only on the upper third of the wall, in a way that kept potential attackers below from seeing them, but also reminded Valerie a bit too much of the training facility windows back in France, where her brother Donovan had spent too many days kicking the shit out of her to make her into the warrior she was today.

And that's just what she was—a warrior. Which was why she had them all gathered like this. She hoped Jackson was okay out there, and she was ready to have this Ella business behind her.

The door creaked.

JUDGMENT HAS FALLEN

She turned with a smile to see Cammie and Sergeant Wallace enter. Glancing around the room, she saw most of them were here. Royland, Duran, Sandra, Diego, and now Cammie and Wallace. That should do.

"Let's begin," Valerie said, doing her best to ignore the sound of the rain as it picked up from droplets to a sudden barrage. "Come on!" she yelled at the window as a gust of wind hit it and caused half the room to jump.

The rest chuckled, nervously, and she realized she'd built this up too much and kept them in suspense for too long.

"Ignoring the storm outside as best I can," she started, "I'm reminded that I cannot and will not ignore the storm that is tearing away at each of us."

Cammie furrowed her brow and said, "Is this a metaphor or simile or one of those things? Because I'll be honest, not my strong suit."

Valerie licked her lips, trying to decide whether Cammie was serious, but went ahead with the cautious route. "Okay, what I'm trying to say is that we've ousted Strake and the CEOs, right? We've left this city in a vacuum of leadership, and the people need a leader. That much is clear."

Royland looked her in the eyes, "They have you."

She smiled at him, noting the bags under his own eyes. They had probably woken him up for this, but she would have to remember to ensure he wasn't taking on too many shifts in the night. Keeping the city safe was important, but it would be hard to keep it safe if her best fighters were all too exhausted to lift a finger.

Unfortunately, her latest decision meant this wasn't her responsibility.

"I'm no leader," Valerie said, making sure to make eye contact with each of them, so they'd know she wasn't saying this out of any sort of cowardice. "You all know that I have been appointed to be this city's Justice Enforcer, and I've come to the conclusion that it only makes sense for me to focus on my own role, while others focus on rebuilding Old Manhattan."

"But you're the one who took out Strake," Duran said, earning him a reproachful look from Cammie.

"No, it's okay," Valerie said to her, then turned to Duran to address his statement. "I removed a source of evil, yes. But do you embrace a spider because it killed a hornet? No, you leave the spider to its web so that it might catch more potentially harmful creatures." Cammie started to raise her hand, but Valerie beat her to it this time. "What I'm trying to say is that there are others better suited to these tasks. Me? I'm here to root out causes of injustice, to make the evil *suffer*, and see that those that do wrong are no longer able to do so."

"Okay, so you want us to step up?" Diego asked. "Is that it? I mean, who amongst us is ready to lead?"

She had been thinking about this question since running back to HQ, and had yet to come up with a perfect answer. But standing here, looking at them, she started to understand.

"You can each play a role. Jackson has his faction, and I'll be counting on him to pull them together while hopefully corralling the rest of the city as best he can. Wallace, you know how the streets work, see that order is maintained on a shallow level while I dole out justice in the deep shadows. Sandra, you are more caring than anyone I know, and these people need to be cared for. You'll be in charge of the medical supplies and more, but you each must work together to ensure this city rises out of darkness to shine with the greatness I know it's capable of."

JUDGMENT HAS FALLEN

Wallace cleared his throat and said, "You trust us? There might be some issues with senior leadership among the police, but I think I have a solution."

"If you feel it's best, then yes." Valerie looked to the rest. "Can I count on you all?"

There was a moment of silence, and then Sandra leaned forward, elbows on the table and said, "Val dear, it sounds like you're planning on leaving us."

One or two sets of eyes in the room went wide with surprise, but the others were apparently sharing this thought.

"That is exactly what I intend to do," Valerie said. "I didn't come here to suddenly be the Queen of New York. I don't *need* to be in the public eye. I just need peace and to see justice has her day. Listen, I have no idea what a proper ruling system is. Have any of us lived in anything other than anarchy, or a dictatorship? No, because that's all this world knows. But what if things weren't always this way? Forget the past, actually. Let's focus on the future and say that, no matter where we've come from, we're focused on what tomorrow brings, and we're going to make damn sure she doesn't bring us crap."

She paused listening to the howling winds and thunderous rain, the worry for Jackson out there hitting her again. Then she sensed another worry, coming from Wallace.

"Where's your partner?" she asked him.

His eyes went wide, but he said, "Missing."

"What do you mean, missing?" Cammie said, turning to him in surprise. "You didn't think that was worth mentioning?"

"Come on, Cammie," Sandra interjected.

"No, if we're going to work together to lead this city like Valerie's saying, this is the type of stuff that can't be kept secret."

SLOAN AND ANDERLE

Wallace held up his hands in surrender, and then slammed them on the table. "For all I know, he's gone off to join his sister."

The room got quiet, aside from the wind and rain.

Finally, Valerie breathed deep and said, "I hope he hasn't. This couldn't have anything to do with the leadership issues you mentioned?"

Wallace snorted in anger, "If it does, I'll get to the bottom of it."

Saying anything more on the matter was likely to piss him off. The feelings from the rest of the room were coming her way too—mostly apprehension, though a different sort of tension was strong between Sandra and Diego. Valerie didn't need her enhanced abilities to sense that one.

"The point is that I trust each of you," Valerie said, bringing the topic back to the right one for the moment.

"You still haven't trusted us by telling us where you'll go," Cammie said.

"I wish I could say I trust you'll lose your attitude someday," Valerie said with a hint of a smile. "But I honestly can't. And maybe that's for the best. As for your question, here's how it is. This city sees me and, while most don't know who I am, the rest either hate me or love me. It's time I went into the shadows."

"Another metaphor?" Cammie asked.

Valerie shook her head as she chuckled. "I mean it quite literally. There are still criminals out there, still vampires on the loose, Nosferatu perhaps. And there's the whole underground rebellion which Ella, and maybe Peterson, are part of. While, yes, staying here appeals to me, the only way I'm going to root them all out and truly make a difference to this town is if it's clear that I'm not running anything, and if I'm

JUDGMENT HAS FALLEN

out there stopping evil before it has a chance to spread."

"And find any ties to the CEOs you can," Duran said with a knowing look.

She touched her nose and then pointed at him. "Exactly."

They lingered to discuss details while the storm raged outside, but just as they were about to conclude the meeting, shouting sounded outside the doors.

Valerie stood and went to the doors where she found two cops holding back Jackson, who was drenched from the rain outside and struggling to break free.

"He's with me," she said, annoyed at the two cops. She didn't know them, or they would've received more of a reprimand for not recognizing him.

Jackson pulled his arms free and glared at the two as they turned to walk off, then ran to Valerie, taking her hands even though the others were watching through the glass doors.

"This is bad," he said. "I couldn't talk my people down, and half have gone off to the underground. They've confirmed Ella's down there, and something big is coming. We've gotta be ready."

"It starts now, then," Valerie said. She stared into his eyes, then pulled him in for a kiss. When she pulled back, his eyes were wide with confusion. "We can't be seen together in the near future, Jackson. It's putting you in danger. It's putting a wall between you and your followers. And it's dangerous for both of us."

"What," his eyes opened larger, if that were possible, "no…."

But she was already walking away from the group and him, back toward the elevators.

"Where are you going?" he asked.

She didn't answer. The others could fill him in on that

SLOAN AND ANDERLE

part of it, and while she was strong and determined in many ways, her little experience with relationships hadn't been enough to prepare her for having to tell the only man she'd ever cared about that she was leaving now.

Instead, she made it to her office and looked it over for a moment. She grabbed her sword and strapped it on, then her pistol. She rifled through her drawer and found any extra ammunition she had stashed. Last, she found her purple jacket, the one he'd helped get mended after the horrible fight that ended with the death of her brother.

Instead of going back out the main way where others could question her and try to stop her, she took the stairs to the pod bay.

Only Sandra stood just outside the doors, waiting for her, sniper rifle slung over her shoulder.

"You know me too well," Valerie said with a sad smile. "But you can't stop me."

"I don't mean to." Sandra looked sideways, bit her lip, and then said, "But can't I come to? You've seen what I'm capable of."

"Yes, from a distance." Valerie stepped over to her friend, putting her hands on her shoulders and then took her in an embrace. A few moments, a few minutes or perhaps it was but a few seconds before she pulled back to look at her again. "You're the best friend a woman could have. When I was a lonely vampire, you made me feel human again, Sandra… but now it's time to be that vampire in the shadows. It's time for me to learn what all this training, and this power from Michael, have made me into."

"For how long?" Sandra asked, her voice quiet.

"It's not like I'm dying." Valerie looked at the doors, feeling anxious. It was like she knew there was trouble, and needed to be out there putting a stop to it. "I'll check in on you, but need to make the message clear that I'm not here to rule this city, just to keep it safe."

"The people you'll be attacking won't think of it as safe." Sandra pulled back, playing with the strap of her rifle. "It's all irrelevant, isn't it?"

"If they want to harm others, then no, it won't be safe for them. But this is how it has to be. This is why the vampires and Weres are with us now, and any that aren't will have to answer to my sword. If they're given the chance to harm, many of them will… and that's bad news for all of us. Regular humans are no different in this regard. All will be judged."

Sandra's eyes flashed with irritation. "You talk like you're some god nowadays, judgment this, justice that. Come on," she pointed to herself, "this is *me* you're talking to."

"And that changes anything?" Valerie sighed. "I've changed, Sandra. I know it's only been a short amount of time in your eyes, but the last few days have been like years as far as I'm concerned. We've learned so much about the world, both this one and the UnknownWorld, that the way we were before… it's long gone."

"The ignorance of youth and all that?" Sandra scoffed. "Okay, sure." She turned to look off to her right.

"I'm not abandoning you, if that's what this is all about."

Sandra looked down at her feet, and then back up to look at her friend. "It sure as hell feels like it."

"Hey, when I come back, and I will, you'll thank me for having set this city on its proper path and we can find some sweets to eat together," she poked her friend, "It will be fun!"

Sandra glared, but she couldn't be angry with Valerie for long, and soon broke into a smile. "Dammit, Valerie. I love you too much to see you hurt. Be careful, will you?"

SLOAN AND ANDERLE

"I can promise to do my best to not get hurt," Valerie said. "But being careful is just about the last thing on my mind right now."

Sandra rested the butt of her rifle on her hip, and raised an eyebrow at her friend, "Oh shut up and just tell me what I want to hear."

Valerie laughed. "I'll be careful."

"See, was that so hard?" Sandra stepped forward and gave her a hug, followed by a quick kiss on each cheek. "I'll miss you."

"Me too."

With that, Sandra smiled, breathed deep, turned and headed back to rejoin the others. She only paused slightly at the elevators to give Valerie one more warning glance as she mouthed *be careful*.

Valerie would miss her and be counting the days between reunions, but right now this was something she had to do. She entered the pod bay and found a Were standing beside the closest pod.

"Who's on their way out?" she asked.

The Were perked up, caught off guard. "Me, but I'm not sure which cop yet." When the Were saw her sword and jacket, his eyes went wide with the realization of who she was. "Is there, ah… something wrong?"

"No, but I'll need you to take me out now, and drop me off half-way to your destination."

"But you don't know where my destination is," he countered.

"Doesn't matter, since I'm not entirely sure where I'm going." She slid into the passenger side of the pod and called out, "Hurry now."

In less than a minute the Were had the pod bay doors

JUDGMENT HAS FALLEN

open, allowing rain to pour in at a forty-five-degree angle and had jumped back in the pod with her..

"You're sure of this?" The Were touched the controls and the pod started to lift off the ground, as it shook with the wind.

"I have a city to protect," she said, and leaned back, closing her eyes. "Wake me when we're there."

CHAPTER FIVE

<u>Enforcer HQ</u>

Jackson stood there in the hallway, completely caught off-guard by what had just happened. He'd come here to be with Valerie, tell her what was happening, and she'd run off on him.

"What the hell just happened?" he asked Wallace who had just walked out to join him.

"It seems our fearless leader is delegating," Wallace said. "It seems you're up for keeping your peeps in line. Trying to pull them back together now that Valerie's out of your way."

Jackson blinked, trying to comprehend this, then cursed and kicked the nearest wall. It didn't help his mood that rain water was dripping down his clothes and he was even wet where the sun didn't shine.

"That might be harder said than done." He leaned with one hand on the wall, staring at the ground. "I've been playing this all wrong, dammit." It all hit him, how he'd been spending so much time with her while his people were just trying to survive. How it must look in their eyes that, not only had they lost someone, but he was courting the woman who led the people who had killed them.

And now, when they'd come to confront him about it, he'd come to her for answers.

It was time he stopped playing around and get back to being the leader he knew he was supposed to be.

He realized Wallace was talking then, but none of the words entered his mind. There was no room for that, now that he knew what he had to do.

His people were waiting for him, so he jogged over to the stairs, ignoring Wallace calling his name behind him, and then took the stairs two at a time until he reached the lobby. Exiting through the glass doors.

He felt like a new man.

Rain swept across him in sheets, but he didn't care.

Hands in the air, he walked into the rain and let it cleanse him. The other factions were leaderless, and instead of reaching out to them and folding them into his own, he'd been blinded by attraction, by his feelings.

Part of him screamed out for Valerie to come back. He wanted to lift her bare body into the air and then fall backward onto her bed with her. Experience her kisses as her hair fell around his face and her shallow breathing told him she was just as excited as he was.

The other part of him felt liberated. For too long he had lost focus, and in a city state like this, where people died if you lost focus, that was unacceptable.

A cop ran past, hands up to block the rain from his glasses, and turned to give him a quizzical look.

"You lost, mate?" the cop asked.

SLOAN AND ANDERLE

"Hardly," Jackson said, then nodded to the man before turning and jogging off into the darkening afternoon.

That's when the explosion sent rubble into the sky with a KA-BOOM!

Jackson stumbled forward, confused, turning for a fight. But all he saw was two forms running away from the smoke and debris—a man and woman who he knew like siblings. The man, Edwardo, caught his gaze and paused, then moved a finger across his neck before pointing at Jackson.

He disappeared, leaving Jackson to turn back to Enforcer HQ and the explosion that had just left the entrance in a pile of rubble. This was his fault—it was an attack by his people, just as they'd attacked before.

Was it him they were after, or Valerie? They obviously hadn't gotten the message yet that Valerie was gone.

And now, so was he.

He took a step back, horrified by the sight of a blue form moving in the chaos. The cop he'd just seen… he was crawling toward the entrance, shouting for help.

Jackson was torn between going back to help him, or running from this place. If they were after him and they saw him running back, they might attack again.

Two Weres appeared from behind the blanket of smoke, then picked up the cop and dragged him inside. More appeared, along with cops fully decked out in riot gear, and they began to form a defensive position.

That was enough for Jackson. This wasn't a place he belonged anymore. Just like Valerie had moved on to bring her battle to the streets, he would move on to lead his people, and all the people he could find, in unity, so that violence like this wouldn't happen again.

If his people would still have him, he'd join back up

with them. Not anyone that had anything to do with this, though—they'd have to be dealt with first.

❖ ❖ ❖

The explosion had thrown Wallace for a loop. He had just about recovered from the surprise at Jackson running off like that, and was turning back to the room where the others sat waiting, when the whole place shook.

The blast was deafening, and his instinct had been to duck to the floor. When he looked up, everything seemed fine except for the thick black smoke joining the rain outside.

Everyone in the room was on the floor too, but a moment later Cammie had sprung into action and was shouting commands. Sandra opened the door and shouted for him, but he nodded and said, "I'm on it!"

He darted to the barracks, snagging four cops along the way, and quickly suited up in riot gear. They each grabbed rifles and pistols, while two of them took riot shields in case they met enemy fire and needed impromptu cover.

"On me!" Wallace roared, then led them out to the lobby and through the debris. The first thing he noticed was a cop crawling toward them, and two Weres going to help him up.

He lifted his rifle to his shoulder, eyes searching their surroundings for the culprit of the attack.

There, across the way, he saw movement. He aimed in, and paused. It was Jackson, staring back at him with a crazed look, and then he was gone.

Could Jackson have had something to do with this? The explosion happened right after he left, and he conveniently was out of harm's way.

But no, he was dating Valerie, it didn't make sense. Or did it? Wallace cursed his confusion.

This wasn't the time to stand around debating with himself. It was the time for action. "You, with me," he said to the closest cop, and only then noticed that it was Karl, the cop who said he'd get his back against the others if it came to that. Good, he needed a cop like him at his side.

The other three took up defensive positions in case there were more attacks, while Wallace and Karl darted across to the side street he had seen Jackson disappear through.

But when they reached it, there was no sign of him. Just rain and streets, and a few druggies poking their heads out of cardboard covers to see what was happening.

Wallace scanned the area, then said, "Fall back."

Karl nodded, and the two started moving back toward HQ. A hand grabbed Wallace's arm and he spun, ready to shoot, but it was just Karl.

"Wait," Karl said.

Wallace looked up at the rain pouring down on them and raised an eyebrow. "You see something?"

"It's not that." Karl glanced around nervously, then back to the entrance of HQ, where cops and Weres had a full defensive position now. "It's Peterson. I overheard the Colonel talking, and…"

"Out with it, Karl."

"They have him, locked up with the former Enforcers."

"Under whose authority?" He ground his teeth. "Don't answer that. Colonel Anderson. I know."

Karl nodded. "I was coming to tell you when the explosion happened."

"Thank you." Wallace put a hand on Karl's shoulder and

made direct eye contact. "You're still with me on this?"

"Until the end," Karl said.

"Good, let's go finish it."

❖ ❖ ❖

Old Manhattan Rooftops

Valerie had just stepped out of the police pod and waved thanks to the cop, and turned to stand below the roof's awning, and debate her next move, when the dim sound of an unnatural explosion reverberated through the night. She immediately stepped out and jumped, grabbing hold of an awning and vaulted herself up and over.

From this higher vantage point, she could turn back toward Enforcer HQ, barely visible in the heavy rain, its blue stripe glowed like a dragon's eye through the haze. Thick, gray smoke rose, adding to the dragon effect.

She cursed herself for leaving so soon, but then realized something. Whoever had attacked would be running away at this point, and likely expect their pursuers to be coming from behind.

It was true that she had no idea where they'd be going, but the simple answer to the dilemma was that Enforcer HQ was by the water, so they couldn't be going that way, and unless they were external operatives, they'd be moving into the city.

With a sinking feeling that made her stomach churn, she thought of her friends back there and hoped to all that was good in this world that they hadn't been hurt.

Because if they had, she had a bad feeling about her ability to differentiate between justice and red-eyed revenge.

SLOAN AND ANDERLE

She glanced around at the buildings between here and HQ, and set up a strategy. If they were running, which she'd bet her left arm they were, they'd likely be at most three or four buildings away by now. At vampire speed and by moving across rooftops, she could reach them at about the five or six buildings away mark, so that's where she set her targets.

With a push using all her strength she ran and leaped from this rooftop to the next one over. Not having had much experience with jumping across roofs before, she yelped as she realized just how strong she was, and how much she'd overcompensated.

She nearly overshot the building, but landed on the far edge of the roof and had to slam into its side, flip over, and grab on to avoid falling. With a grunt, she pulled herself back up and was happy to see just a small jump to the next building over.

The next groups of buildings provided more of a challenge, as some were taller and some were shorter, but she continued throwing herself from one to the next, sometimes climbing up fire escapes and once having to run into the building and make her way to the roof.

When she hit the area close to her target, she ran to the edge and looked down. Of course, she'd known it wouldn't be that easy—but a woman can hope.

The next step was to leap along the buildings at an outward diagonal, and then zigzag back. It was a chore, but her anger drove her on. She was about to make her third jump, when her enhanced hearing picked up footsteps that were moving louder and faster than regular ones, and she turned to see two shadows disappear around a corner.

Definitely, she thought as she ran and leaped.

"Holy cow-balls!" she screamed as she fell, but she was

JUDGMENT HAS FALLEN

ready, and at the next building she kicked off of it, not realizing that kick would put a big dent in the bricks the way it did, or that she might slip like she did.

Now she was falling head first, but the kick had sent her in the right direction. She grabbed hold of a balcony railing as she fell past, grunted as her arm was nearly yanked from its socket, and then twisted to jump to the next one down, and then again to the ground.

Not even waiting to see how far off they were, she pushed out in anger, so that a wave of terror spread out around her. Shrieks came from the nearby apartment buildings, and she heard what sounded like a body colliding with a garbage can.

Following the sound, she sprinted down the alley and turned to come into another one. She saw them. One man was helping up a woman, both glancing around with eyes full of terror.

She didn't even bother to run now, because as she drew close, they collapsed to their knees in their own puddles of piss.

"You," she said, and then drew her sword and pointed at them, "are responsible for the explosion at Enforcer HQ. Am I wrong?"

"It wasn't us!" the woman said, and a wave of negativity pushed out from her.

Lies.

"Once more I ask…" Valerie stepped closer, pushing on the element of fear. "Are you guilty?"

The man whimpered, and then tried to stand and charge her. She didn't even flinch, just simply moved her sword so that he impaled himself on it.

"Guilty," the man said, trying to spit on her as his life faded.

SLOAN AND ANDERLE

She kicked him off of her sword, then looked to the woman. "I've come to bring justice to this land. The wanton death of innocents is unacceptable. And while none of us are truly innocent, the point remains." She lifted her sword and let the fear fade so she could see the woman's true emotions. "Guilty, or not?"

"Eat shit and die on your own puke, you freak of natu—" The woman's words choked off as Valerie's sword sliced through her neck.

"I'll accept that as a guilty plea," she said, and then turned so she wouldn't have to watch the body fall over with a plop on the wet cement.

Footsteps approaching.

She knelt to clean her sword and then, in one smooth motion, sheathed the sword and ducked into the shadows and walked away.

It wasn't until she was a half a block away that she heard the first shriek. Spreading terror through the city wasn't her intention, but if word reached the other perpetrators and they got the message before justice had to come calling?

Perhaps that would be for the best.

She stopped to lean against a wall. In spite of the heavy rain, this alley still smelled heavily of piss, but she just wrapped her arms around herself and ignored it.

Imparting justice wasn't easy, and she felt her nerves causing her arms to shake. A life was a life, but when that life was trying to harm others, it was forfeit. She didn't see any way around this fact.

But that didn't mean she'd have to like it.

She steeled herself, shook it off, and continued into the shadows to figure out her next move.

CHAPTER SIX

Enforcer HQ

Wallace stood with his arms folded, fuming as he waited for Karl to return with the keys, but that anger got even worse when he saw Sgt. Cline walking back with him.

"What's the meaning of this?" Sgt. Cline demanded. "The Colonel had him locked up, you don't—"

A solid punch to the nose dropped Cline back and onto his butt. Wallace knelt beside him, finger in the man's face. "I was appointed by Valerie after she liberated this city. To hear you talk like an ungrateful little boot licker tells me one thing, you've turned against me and the new command. Which means you belong in this cell."

"Bull!" Sgt. Cline shook his head and tried to push himself back up.

Wallace reached out and shoved him right back down. "Karl, grab the keys." Sgt. Cline opened his mouth to argue,

SLOAN AND ANDERLE

but Wallace rolled his eyes and pulled out his pistol, aiming it at the man's knee. "Any day, Karl."

"You're a Sergeant," Cline said. "Not some dictator of this place!"

"By the power appointed to me by Valerie, I give you the right to shut the hell up."

Cline growled and moved to strike, but before he could move a step closer, Karl brought a knife-hand to the man's throat, dropping him to the ground in a coughing fit.

For a moment, he looked at Wallace sheepishly, but when Wallace nodded approvingly, the young cop beamed.

"Glad to have you with me," Wallace said as Karl tossed over the keys. They went to the fourth room on the left, where Karl's snooping had revealed Peterson would be, and quickly worked the lock.

"You better not be naked doing weird things to yourself in there," Wallace called out, then pulled the door open.

"Taking your time, I see," Peterson said. He looked like crap, only wearing a white T-shirt and his cop pants, no shoes or anything else.

"Honestly?" Wallace frowned. "I kind of thought you'd left us to go with Ella."

"Partner." Peterson took Wallace in a handshake and then a hug. "I would never dream of abandoning you to this hell hole alone. I told you that."

Wallace introduced Karl, and kicked the other cop on the floor in the ribs as he passed, but then froze at the turn in the hallway.

Colonel Anderson stood tall with Major Donnoly and Buland at either side, a dozen more cops behind them.

"So it's happening now?" Wallace asked. "This is it?"

"This is it," Anderson said with a nod. But Donnoly's eyes

shifted, and Wallace knew he wasn't fully on board.

Perhaps this could work after all.

"Colonel Anderson," Wallace stood tall, hands behind his back, one folded into the other, "in the time of Commander Strake, you were his man, were you not?"

"How dare you?" The Colonel's nostrils flared.

"There was no one else between him and the police force, I'm quite certain of this fact. So certain, because I remember quite vividly seeing the two of you dining together on a number of occasions."

"I am your superior officer," Colonel Anderson said, hand on his pistol. "You think I'd stand by and let a lowly Sergeant run things?" He laughed and motioned to the cops behind him. "Throw him in with the rest. Him and his two friends."

"I do not hand over authority," Wallace said, his voice full of such command that the others halted in their advance. "Not to you, anyway."

Anderson's eyes narrowed.

The other cops looked around, confused.

"There's not a cop on the force who would vouch for your honor," Wallace said to the Colonel. "Major Donnoly, however, is a prime example of what it means to serve on the force." He turned to Major Donnoly and nodded, hoping with all his body and soul that this man would make the right move here. "You, sir, are why I became a cop to begin with. It was your speech at Capital Square, on the city's twenty-fifth anniversary of having rebuilt, that I knew I'd one day wear the blue."

"Enough ass-kissing here," Anderson said, but then Donnoly held up a hand, cutting him off.

"Let the man finish," Donnoly said, and the Colonel stared at him like he'd just eaten his firstborn, but didn't speak.

SLOAN AND ANDERLE

"You, sir, have honor," Wallace continued, "and that's why I will peacefully hand over command, as appointed to me by Valerie and all of her kind, what we've now come to know as the UnknownWorld, and the authority for which their kind represents. I will hand over command, but to you alone. Provided the other members of the force agree, and Colonel Anderson resigns."

"What a preposterous proposal," Anderson said, scoffing. "I'll have your throat torn out, you little—"

"Agreed." Donnoly gave a nod to the cops behind them and said, "Take Grady Anderson into custody and see that he either resigns or is thrown behind bars. He no longer holds the rank of Colonel here."

"You little piece of rat puke," Anderson reached for his pistol, but two cops standing next to him moved in and pinned him to the wall, while a third took his pistol and arc rod. "This is mutiny, you'll all hang. I'll see to it that your mother's look upon their son's lifeless eyes, I'll—"

Wallace interrupted him with a punch to the nose. As the man fell limp in the other cops' hands, Wallace took off the rank insignia and handed it to Donnoly.

"I look forward to serving you, *Colonel* Donnoly." The others were all looking between the three men, unsure, but when Donnoly accepted the insignia and removed his old ones, the tension eased.

"What are you waiting for?" Donnoly asked the two men still holding Anderson. "Remove him for debriefing, and then let him make his choice. I'll be along to see to him shortly."

As they dragged the defeated former Colonel away, Donnoly turned to Wallace with a puzzled look on his face.

"You're sure about this?" he asked. "I pegged you wrong, apparently. Thought you'd put up a fight."

JUDGMENT HAS FALLEN

"Sir, I was a street cop." Wallace clasped Peterson on the shoulder, who nodded approvingly. "Me and my partner here. I've only ever wanted to be out there serving the people, and we must all play to our comparative advantage."

Donnoly nodded. "You realize that, in this new climate, you'll never be *just* a street cop. Not anymore."

"As long as I can play the part, I'm happy to serve additionally in whatever capacity you see fit, sir."

"Very well, consider your reassignment in effect as of this moment." He looked around at the rest of them, then started walking off in the direction the other two had taken Anderson. "The rest of you on me. We have to be ready in case that bastard Anderson has a card or two up his sleeves."

When it was over, Peterson rubbed his head and stared at Wallace in awe. "I don't know what the hell that was, but, damn."

Karl looked back the way the police went with Anderson, "I thought there'd be blood for sure," he murmured.

"Hopefully not wishing for it though, right?" Wallace asked.

Karl turned to look at him, "No, sir."

"Good. Remember that blood isn't the only answer, and often isn't the best. I wasn't meant for leadership, or not the administrative type anyway. Most of the string pulling is done out of the spotlight, after all."

"Is Valerie going to like this?" Peterson asked.

"She's gone into the shadows herself," Wallace said. "She's out there, your sister is out there… I thought it only fitting that we get ourselves out there too."

"That's why I love having you as a partner," Peterson

said with a chuckle. "And you," he said to Karl, "I have you to thank for finding me?"

Karl nodded.

Peterson smiled and nodded toward the doors. "There's not a rule about patrols being limited to two in a partnership. Come on."

"You mean it?" Karl asked, looking between the two men, a smile on his face.

"Hey, if he says it, he means it." Wallace laughed. "Let's go out there and serve the people."

"Don't you think we ought to brief Valerie on this?" Peterson asked.

"Ah, you wouldn't have heard yet," Wallace said, still having a hard time believing the words as he said, "she's gone. Come on, I'll explain on the way."

❖ ❖ ❖

Jackson's Restaurant

Jackson was practically soaked right through by the time he reached the restaurant his uncle had operated for over thirty years, the same restaurant where he knew he'd find his top leaders at. Rain had soaked through even to his underwear, and his toes sloshed in his boots.

Not even bothering to apologize for his appearance, he walked right past Bill the waiter and went to the backroom. It was a good thing he'd eaten recently, or the scent of almond crusted lamb would've been damn tempting. He pushed aside the yellow-beaded curtain at the back of the room and then proceeded to descend the stairs beyond it.

At the bottom of the stairs, half a dozen men and

women stood in the center of a large room, a couple dozen more at the bar on the far wall, and several more lounging about on the couches.

As always, a pleasant melody played from the grand piano in the corner, where the twins he'd hired took turns at the keys.

He took a step toward the small group in the room's center and the woman, wearing a long, green dress that complimented her wavy red hair, turned to him and nearly snarled.

"Look what the storm so graciously tossed our way," she said.

"Morgan! Always a pleasure." He stopped approximately two strides away from them, and noticed his left arm was twitching involuntarily. Annoying, given the timing. "Do you have any idea the shit-storm you've just bit into?"

Morgan just frowned. "I have no idea what you just said."

The others in the center of the room had turned to him now too. They were glancing amongst themselves nervously, and whispering about him, he was sure.

"The bombing at Enforcer HQ," Jackson said. "Who was it?"

Morgan just stared at him, giving nothing away.

"Fine, I don't need to know." He paced the room, making eye contact with each of the leaders. "But know this. There will be a reckoning."

"You threaten us with stories of the undead?" a female voice said, one he was sure he recognized but wasn't sure where from. When he turned to the couches, he saw her there, sitting on a footstool in the center.

Ella.

She looked different without a uniform on. Here she wore jeans with a long black coat over a green sweater, and her hair, normally pulled up in a bun, hung around her shoulders.

"So this is where you've taken to hiding?" Jackson asked, glaring.

"Hiding?" She stood finishing her glass of beer and handing it to a man sitting nearby. "No, I wouldn't say that. Filling a seat while you were gone is more like it. Problem is, the seat has grown mighty comfortable. I'm not sure I feel like giving it back."

"I'm going to assume you're talking about that footstool back there, because any sort of metaphor that refers to my leadership being challenged will not end well for you."

"You sound confident, for one who's been sleeping with the enemy." Her smile was a mischievous one, and when the whispers and suspicious glances his way picked up again, he knew she'd told them everything.

"So you don't deny it?" Morgan said, moving to stand beside Ella. "You've not only been siding with the people who killed our dear friends, Ackers and Wilson among them, but… you've slept with this monster? This abomination?"

"We attacked her, she defended herself." He assessed the room, looking for any allies. Judging by the looks on their faces, it was going to be a tough crowd. "That's all there is to it."

Morgan scoffed. "And why should we believe you?"

"Because it's true," a new voice said, soft and high pitched.

They all turned to see Lorain, the teenage fighter who Valerie had confronted Jackson about after first learning he was Mercer. Lorain stood tall at the bar, several young men around her—young men who, Jackson hoped, would jump to defend her if needed.

"What do you know of it, girl?" Ella asked.

"No, stay out of it," Morgan said to Lorain. "Sit back down

JUDGMENT HAS FALLEN

and shut your trap."

"I won't." Lorain came over to stand beside Jackson, and he was glad to see that at least two of the young men stepped forward as well, even if not all the way. "She's not this monster you have all been making her out to be. I met her, and she spared my life. It wasn't like she was out for a blood-bath, and she certainly wasn't sucking blood and flying through the air like some of the bullshit stories I've heard this night."

"Tell that to the families of Ackers and Wilson!" a man in the back shouted, and Morgan beamed.

"Point me in the right direction and I will," Jackson said.

Lorain nodded. "Me too. I'm not afraid, because it's the truth. Valerie was caught in the middle of our battle, and to her, we were the attackers! We took out several of the faction leaders, and others are on the run. That was our goal, was it not? And we knew there would be repercussions."

"Ackers especially knew this," Jackson chimed in, noticing the shake in the girl's voice. She was being brave, but it took an effort. "And to set this straight, we have Valerie to thank for removing Strake, for giving us the freedom to set this city right again. To make it great, like it once was."

"Who says it was ever great?" Ella motioned around to those in the room. "Has anyone here ever seen it great? No, we live wondering when we'll be attacked again, whether from the inside or outside. Who the hell knows. There are druggies who are lost to us, children who've seen more torment than we'll ever experience in a lifetime. Make it great?" She laughed. "Maybe you're talking of the days before the great collapse, huh? This mythical world where everything was hunky-dory and the streets were made of fucking gold? Well I don't buy it! I say we make it great on our terms, and I can damn well assure you, that doesn't include allowing vampires

SLOAN AND ANDERLE

and werewolves to roam the streets!"

"YEAH!" a chorus went up in agreement. Others pounded the bar with their glasses, while a couple stood, hands on weapons.

Jackson glanced over at Lorain with a look that said to be ready to run, but held up his hands for silence.

"Who do you think you're talking to here?" he asked. "I've led you against the other seven factions of this city, seen you fed when Strake and his Enforcers, to include Ella here, I might add, did their best to keep us down. A foot pushes you into the mud, but the minute that foot lets up, you roll over to kiss it?"

The crowd muttered. A couple nodding in agreement. Good—this could work.

"If you can't trust me, you can't trust anyone." He turned to the eldest man in the circle, who he'd known since he was a boy. "Talden, how long have we been at this?"

"Too damn long," the old man hacked.

"All that time, you've been like a father to me."

"And you, a son to me," the old man said. His weary, blue eyes stared back, intensely, and then he turned to the crowd and said, "I stand with Jackson Mercer!"

The room erupted in new murmurs, and people stood, some moving over to stand by Jackson, others by Ella. More were coming to Jackson's side, however, and he was just starting to feel confident when the back door rattled, followed by three kicks and a pound of a fist. *Emergency*.

"Get the door," Jackson said, feeling his voice go horse as he said it. This was not the best time for emergencies.

Baxter the bartender, a large man with a widow's peak and thick sideburns, grabbed an old arc rod he must've taken from an enforcer at one point, and went for the door. He opened it, but quickly stood aside.

"It's just the boys," he said, nodding to Jackson.

"Not quite," one of the teenage boys said as he entered, holding a bag. Three other boys, also in their teens, followed and were dragging two larger bags. No, not bags, sheets. Bloody, rain-drenched sheets.

"What the hell is this?" Talden said.

Morgan, ever eager to make the first move, stepped up and took the bag in spite of the boy's protestation. But when she looked inside, she dropped it and stepped back with a gasp.

The bag fell open and a head rolled out, stopping to face Jackson.

Not just any head, the head of his old friend, Edwardo. He knew without having to ask what was in the sheets.

"We found them along the retreat path," one of the boys said. "Didn't know what to do, so we broke into the nearest house and just took these sheets. I mean, we couldn't just leave them there, right?"

The room was silent, until finally Talden stepped forward and put an arm around the boy. "You did right."

"They shouldn't have been in this position to begin with," Baxter said. At the looks he received for that, he held up the arc rod pointing it around the room. "I said so, didn't I? I said Jackson would be back, and that we needed to trust him. That he wouldn't lead us astray."

"He slept with the enemy!" Morgan said, practically spitting as she spoke. "I'd say that's a bit of a vested interest right there."

"She's not the enemy!" Lorain spat back.

"ENOUGH!" Jackson took the bag and covered the head at his feet. "I'm going to assume these two were responsible for the bombing on Enforcer HQ?"

"There were a few more responsible than just those two," Baxter said with a pointed look at Morgan and Ella. "That Enforcer's been getting all in their heads."

"Then they've been judged and found guilty," Jackson said, massaging his temple as he said it. He put his hands back at his side and stood tall. "This is a new world, not the one you all knew just a week and a half ago. This is a world where, if you harm others, or intend to harm others, you will face justice."

"And where's their justice?" Morgan shouted. "They didn't deserve this!"

"Who did then, Morgan?" He pointed at Ella. "Or maybe you? Something tells me a lot more heads will roll before this is over, and I can tell you right now, those heads won't belong to anyone else on my team. If you were involved with this attack, and by that I mean you were aware and supported it in any way, I want you out of here, now."

Several standing near Morgan glanced at each other nervously, but she stood her ground. "You've abandoned your people. This is what your actions led to!" She pointed at the bodies.

"Wrong," Talden said, stepping up beside Jackson and standing tall. "They listened to you, Morgan. That was their mistake."

"Just like any that go with you now will, I'm certain, find that to be a mistake."

"We'll have vengeance for this," Ella said, moving for the door. "Come, Morgan, we're done with these lovers of vampires and Weres."

Morgan looked about to hesitate, but when Baxter flicked on his arc rod, she moved to follow Ella. When they were

JUDGMENT HAS FALLEN

gone, a handful of others followed, but they left the bodies where they were, for Jackson's people to deal with.

Baxter grunted and slid the door shut, secured it, and then turned back to the room, waiting.

Talden cleared his throat, and said, "Boys, we'll have a burial for them. But for now, get 'em outside. Baxter, get Jackson here a drink."

"My pleasure," Baxter said, moving back to his spot behind the bar.

"You were gone a few days," Talden said as he and Jackson moved to the bar. The others were hovering around as if not sure whether joining in the conversation was the right move or not.

"She's not bad," Jackson said, referring to Valerie. They didn't all get it, he could tell by the unsure looks in their eyes.

"If you say so, boss," Baxter said, handing two whiskies to the men on the other side of the bar.

"But with Ella out there stirring up trouble," Talden said, shaking his head, "we're bound to need all the help we can get. When she had Morgan on her side, I knew there was more to all this. But vampires? Weres?"

"It's all real, dammit." He tilted back his head and downed the whiskey. It burned and tasted of cinnamon, but after that near explosion with Morgan and Ella, he needed it. "She wouldn't admit it if you asked, and I shouldn't be saying anything… but the cat's out of the bag, isn't it?"

"Cat, sir?" Baxter asked, puzzled.

Jackson waved the comment off. "I mean, Ella kind of said everything already, so there're no secrets being revealed here, right?"

"Doesn't mean we believed it," Talden said.

"As much as I tried to make them," Lorain chimed in,

reaching for a glass of whiskey. Baxter promptly slid the glass away from her, then offered it to the next person over. She glared.

"Give the girl a break," Jackson said. "She's one of the very few willing to go head to head with Morgan for me. If that doesn't get you a drink, I don't know what will."

"Did you… actually sleep with the vampire?" a man to Jackson's left asked, earning him a whack over the counter from Baxter.

"You know that's none of our business," Baxter said, but couldn't help giving Jackson a curious look.

"As you said," Jackson replied, shaking his head. "I'm not here to spread rumors or kiss and tell. I'm here to see that my people are safe, which, apparently, they aren't. Anyone running around with Ella right now's in trouble. She's a loose cannon, a half-cocked pistol ready to explode in your face if you pull that trigger. And now that Valerie's on the prowl…"

"Care to explain that one?" Talden said, taking a sip from his whiskey. He licked his upper lip, likely a nervous twitch more than to ensure he got every drop of the liquor.

"When we planned the attack on Enforcer HQ, just after Strake had been ousted, we knew we were dealing with the supernatural," Jackson said. "That wasn't new for most of us." He glanced over at Lorain who, he knew had doubted the existence of the supernatural until only recently. Some in the city knew, especially those that hid in the shadows and lived underground. Others managed to stay sheltered. "What none of us knew, was how powerful she was."

"So the fights that night…?" Talden leaned into the bar, resting on one elbow as he finished the whiskey. "It was what we suspected?"

"An internal war, yes. Vampire versus vampire, and the

good side won." Jackson scooted his glass toward Baxter and nodded for him to fill it up. "Let me tell you, she's out of this world." He laughed, realizing how true that was. "But I mean, her power is like nothing we've ever seen, and we're damn lucky to have her on our side. Morgan and Ella, and the rest who went with them?" He sighed, watching Baxter pour the brown liquid into his glass. "If they follow this path, I doubt very much we'll be seeing them again… alive, anyway."

"I won't let any harm come to Morgan," Talden said, and his knuckles were white from gripping the glass.

Jackson looked at the old man, and nodded. He knew all about the old flame this man carried for Morgan, a life long ago left behind, but not the memories of it. Whether Morgan felt the same or not was never clear, but few didn't know of Talden's love for her. In fact, Jackson was quite surprised the old man's feelings hadn't clouded his judgment in their current predicament.

It was just one more testament to the man's character.

"Then we'll have to get her back to our side, and quick." Jackson accepted the drink from Baxter and stood, glass raised. "To new beginnings, to survival, and to bringing us back together, in unity."

The room roared, some cheering and others stamping their feet. They had their leader back, Jackson was with his people again. Aside from that gaping hole in his heart that yearned for Valerie.

He felt at home again.

CHAPTER SEVEN

Old Manhattan Streets

Valerie's first instinct after passing judgment on the people who had bombed Enforcer HQ was to rush back and check on everyone. If any of them were hurt, she'd be devastated. If Sandra, Jackson, or Diego were hurt, she'd tear this city a new asshole.

She leaped along the buildings until she reached a good vantage point, and then sighed with relief. The fortifications she'd had the Weres put up around Enforcer HQ had kept the damage to a minimum. Yes, the doors had been blown off, and the glass walls, but that was to be expected. From what she could see, there was no blood and there weren't any body parts strewn about, and it was entirely feasible that no one had been harmed.

Her insides clenched with the thought that maybe she passed judgment too fast. Maybe the two she'd killed didn't deserve death?

JUDGMENT HAS FALLEN

But no, she shook that thought aside as fast as she could. They had tried to kill her and everyone she loved. Their intent was harm, murder, destruction, and she couldn't be double-guessing justice in these situations. To do so would mean a stall in terms of the progress of this city.

Several police pods came zooming around the side of the building, likely heading out to look for any sign of their attackers and set up a perimeter to look for any second wave attacks.

As one passed overhead, a strange feeling of warmth and comfort swept over Valerie, and she knew, though she didn't understand how she knew, that Sandra was in that pod.

She was tempted to follow it, but knew the protocol—when they found nothing, they'd return to HQ and figure out a way to ensure such an attack never happened again. They'd regroup, send out soldiers into the streets, and discuss ways to stop the underground movement against them.

Only they no longer needed to have such discussions. Valerie was taking care of that. She was the Justice Enforcer, and would pull the rotting weeds from this city.

But first, she figured it was time for a drink.

Not because she was thirsty, but because she only now realized how draining the pursuit of those two had been, in addition to leaping across buildings to reach this spot.

She'd filled the secret pockets of her jacket with small vials of blood, and now reached in and pulled one out. Holding it up to the light, she watched how it coated to the nearly indestructible glass.

It was a vile act, drinking blood, but one she'd come to not only be fine with, but enjoy. The way it moved through her reminded her of the way Jackson's fingers felt as he gently ran them up and down her back.

SLOAN AND ANDERLE

If only Jackson's touch had the healing ability blood had, she'd just keep him around at all times. She laughed at the thought of him hanging around during fights so that he could caress her skin and heal her, but it was a silly thought. She drank the vial in two sips, and then placed it in her coat for later.

This time, instead of leaping from the building and using up energy, she took the stairs. She'd been in a hurry to get out here on the streets and make a difference, but now that she was here, she realized she didn't know exactly where to start.

She gave herself a little extra push to get down the stairs faster, but nothing that would drain her.

At the bottom she glanced around at the night, appreciating the light drizzle that had replaced the torrential downpour. She was soaked, and so decided she had a starting point.

The red door—Jackson's uncle.

She made her way over to Capital Square and knocked, but there was no response. A glance back showed that the square was quite crowded, in spite of the rain, and she decided it would be a good idea to simply walk among the people. Not many of them recognized her, she imagined, and there'd be so many people it would be hard to pick her out of the crowd.

About half-way down the street and toward the square, she stopped at a familiar smell of meat. The hot dog vender was there, just getting his grill going, with a large umbrella canopy overhead.

Smart.

Jackson had offered this man money for information that first time she'd met Jackson. Money for information.

It was worth a try.

She fished around in her pockets and found the secret

one where she'd put the main stash of coins from Commander Strake's office.

Taking out a couple of the copper ones, she approached and slid them into his money tray.

The man, in a long raincoat and wearing a cap, glanced up at her with curiosity. "Either you're buying dogs for a party, or you're in the wrong place."

"I was with Jackson before, Jackson Mercer."

He pursed his lips at that and cocked his head. "And that makes us best friends?"

"I'm a nice person to have on your friend list."

He considered that, and then smiled wide as he pocketed the money. "Haven't seen him."

"I have. But that's not why I'm here."

"What is it then?" His hand went to the money in his pocket, as if debating whether it was worth keeping. "There's been talk of trouble lately, the kind I'm not sure I need."

"Exactly why I'm here. What sort of trouble?"

He frowned, flipped a couple hotdogs, and then breathed out as he made up his mind. "I've heard of you. We all have."

"What've you heard?"

He glanced at the money tray, and she slapped another coin down.

"Word on the street is you play with dark magic, the kind that'll bring up demons in the night."

She nearly laughed at that. "So this is a witch hunt now?" She shook her head. "Not good enough. I wanna know where I can find the people talking. I need to know where people like that hang out, and," she leaned in, lowering her voice, "if you know anything about a blood trade, I wanna hear about that, as well."

He scrunched his nose at the last one, and she figured

that was enough to know he wasn't versed in the vampire ways or the hunt for their blood. She'd put a stop to it, as far as she knew, but she had to ensure it wasn't still being bought and sold.

If it was, the people who wanted it would soon want more, and when there's a short supply, people get dangerous.

But she meant to cut it off early and make sure anyone involved was out of her city.

"Can't help you with blood," he said. "Though a word of wisdom from me to you is that, if you go talking about that stuff, the demon rumors are only gonna grow stronger."

She nodded, "And the source of information?"

He sighed. "I shouldn't be saying nothing, but since you and Mercer are buddy-buddy, I'll let this one slide." His eyes darted from side to side, and then he lowered his voice as he pulled a couple of hotdogs from the grill, placing them in their buns.

"I promise, I can be discreet," she said.

"You didn't hear this from me," he handed her one of the hotdogs, then smothered it with catsup for her. "They say there's a woman in the bar with the green door, across the square. You want answers, you go to her."

Valerie frowned. "Please tell me you're not talking about Cammie."

His eyes went wide. "You know her?"

"Give me my money back."

"Hold on, hold on." He held up his hands. "You wanted answers about all this, I'm telling you names I've heard and where to find them."

"Tell me more than just the one, and maybe we can stay friends."

He looked at her nervously and nodded. "If the rumors

about you are true, you're not going to scare off from venturing into the darker parts of town, are you?"

She shook her head and assessed the hotdog, then took a bite.

"Good, right?" he said.

She just nodded and chewed, waiting.

"The best in all the city," he said with a smile. "Just like this intel I'm about to give you… but let's just say your payment hardly covers it. I tell you this because we're such close friends."

She swallowed her food and said, "Indeed."

"You don't want to be hanging out in the crowded parts of town for what you're after. Go up to the old graveyard, used to be part of what was Central Park, back in the old world. There, you just gotta be smart and you might get lucky."

"You have a name for me?" she asked.

He shook his head. "I really wish I did. That's not a part of town I venture into… though I've heard rumors of a place they call *The Cat's Eye*. You find that place, I imagine you'll have all the answers you're looking for."

"Thank you," she said, and turned to leave.

"The hotdog's on the house," he said. "Just, you know, in case you were thinking about paying for it."

She turned back to him, smiled and took another bite before walking off into the darkness.

CHAPTER EIGHT

Over the Streets of Old Manhattan

The streets had their normal people milling about, with nothing out of the ordinary as far as Sandra could see from the back of the police pod. She'd brought her sniper rifle and was ready in case they thought they found the people responsible for the attack on Enforcer HQ, but she knew it was a long shot.

What a time for Valerie to decide to fight the war by herself, Sandra thought. It peeved her that Valerie hadn't come back to check on her, and that she didn't have her best friend with her through this.

True, they'd been more like master and slave for much of their relationship, but Sandra had never really seen it that way.

"I'm still totally confused," Peterson said, driving while Wallace and Sandra looked out the pod windows. "Who's in charge of this city?"

JUDGMENT HAS FALLEN

"Right now it's a bit like a board of directors," Wallace said. "We have Donnoly taking charge of the police—"

"Because you handed over the reins, even though Valerie gave you control?"

"Right. Me taking control at the time made sense, but this was the only way to get Anderson out of the way."

"That corrupt son of a bitch," Peterson growled. "But Jackson and the factions?"

"As far as I can tell, Jackson's out there working that angle now," Sandra said. "At least, that's what I gathered. Then we have Royland keeping the vampires in check, Cammie, the Weres, with the help of Duran and Victor, who take the shifts out on patrols. I'm not sure we need one main leader, at least not yet. While we figure out this city, it makes sense to keep it organized by separate parts… at least, I think so."

"Who made you the City State expert?" Peterson asked. "No offense, I'm genuinely wondering where this is coming from."

"No, I mean, I know as little as the rest of you all, when it comes to actual experience." She paused, thinking she might have seen something moving in the shadows below, but then it was gone. Possibly Valerie? She shook it off, ignoring it. "Back in France, there was a lot of downtime. My role was basically to serve the vampires, train in combat in case they needed me, occasionally let them feed on me and—"

"Hold the fuck up," Wallace said. "Occasionally you let them *feed* on you?"

She felt her cheeks blush with annoyance. "Yes, that's what I said. I was happy to help my masters heal, and—"

"MASTERS?"

"Will you shut the hell up so I can finish my story?" She stopped watching outside and flicked him in the ear—a little something she'd learned from Valerie. "Yes, damn, they were my masters, and fed on me. Get over it. Valerie let me drink of her blood too and, stop, before you interrupt me, it was beautiful. Something you'll never understand. And it healed me too, kept me young, and what I was *trying* to say was that there was a lot of downtime, but there are some in France who pride themselves on discussing what the City States of Europe will evolve into as recovery proceeds. I spent a lot of time reading all the papers I could get a hold of, propaganda you could call it, that went on and on about the best way to rule the people. So I picked up some of it, and began to form my own opinions."

"So you had time to think between blood-feeding sessions," Wallace said, grossed out. "I'm starting to wonder if maybe Ella isn't so wrong here."

"Hey," Peterson pulled the pod over to a stopping point, lowering it so it hovered ten feet off the ground between two buildings. "She's my sister and I love her, but we've chosen our side, and she betrayed our trust by running off like that. You want to join her and fight *against* Valerie, get the hell out right now."

Wallace looked at him with a frown, then back to Sandra. He raised his eyebrows and tried to laugh, but it was forced. "Sorry, you're right. It's just, how could she feed on you, Sandra? That doesn't sit right with me."

"It was a different time, and honestly, a different Valerie." Sandra turned back to staring out the window, where ahead she could see the bright yellow and purple lights of Capital Square in the distance. "Back then, none of us knew what being a vampire truly meant. A lot of us thought they really were creatures of evil, like the legends say. It was only after being with her for a couple of years that I began to see the softer side of her, the side that wasn't torn apart by being separated from her old, human life. The side that took me in as a friend and… maybe more."

"You're saying you two were lovers?" Peterson looked to Wallace. "She did just imply that, right?"

"No, jackass," Sandra flicked his ear again, and Wallace laughed. "I'm saying, the feeding, it was like a bond we held, linking us together in this beautiful, *non-sexual*, sort of way. Although…"

"Yes?" Peterson looked back, waiting anxiously.

"We might've kissed once."

"Ah, I knew it!" Peterson laughed, beaming with a wide smile in Wallace's direction.

"Why does that make you happy?" Sandra asked, completely bewildered.

"It's hot, right?" Peterson laughed. "Come on, the idea of you and her, lips pressed together, and—"

Now it was Wallace's turn to flick Peterson in the ear, and he did it, hard.

"Ow!" Peterson held his ear, the smile gone. "The hell was that for?"

"Um, you do realize you're basically having a sexual fantasy about Sandra, who is sitting right there, and Valerie, who not only has a thing going with Jackson, but is kind of like our boss? It's wrong on so many levels, man."

"Oh…" Peterson's face went pale and he turned back to Sandra. "Shit, I'm so sorry. I didn't mean it like that."

She just laughed. "Hey, you can sexually fantasize about me all day long, I couldn't give a rat's ass. But just remember that it's not going to happen for one, and that Diego's my man and happens to be a Were who could kick your butt into next Tuesday."

SLOAN AND ANDERLE

"Where the hell'd you learn all these American sayings anyway?" Wallace asked, clearly trying to change the subject. "I mean, rat's ass, kick your butt into next Tuesday… those aren't things people say in France, are they?"

She shrugged. "Well now we're moving on to that? Tell you what, get us back to HQ, this is a bust. I'll tell you all about it on the way. But the simple answer—more reading. There aren't really books anymore, except some children's book I found lying around, but there's the papers people write and…" She blushed at the next part.

Peterson was turning the pod around and making it rise higher in the air, but he turned around. "What?"

"I might have come across some letters a woman from here had been writing to a captain of one of those trading blimps. Love letters."

"You learned American idioms from someone's love letters? And that included rat's ass?"

She laughed. "I never said they had a perfect relationship… at least, from what I could gather from the notes."

Peterson laughed, but then Wallace said, "WATCH OUT!" and Peterson stopped abruptly so that he could steer the pod away from slamming into one of the buildings.

"Let's save the stories until we're safely away from this guy's driving," Wallace said.

"Agreed," Sandra said, and returned to staring out the window in silence, watching the buildings with their bright lights passing below, wondering about the rest of the world with its lack of power. With so much here, it was amazing they hadn't figured out a way to spread it back out to those in need yet.

But then again, there were much larger problems than a little extra light at night.

JUDGMENT HAS FALLEN

The ride back went smoothly, and soon they were back in the pod bay. She exited just as another pod pulled in, and when Cammie got out they compared notes. It turned out that no one else had spotted anything from the air.

"Same here," Diego said as he approached, the metal doors sliding shut behind him. "We went out on the ground, but nada. Only… a few blocks away we found blood. Picked them up with my enhanced smell to find it the first time. I tried to pick up more, like a lingering scent of vampire, perhaps, but no such luck."

"The blood, was it human?" Sandra asked.

He shrugged. "Valerie's great at making that differentiation, but not me. I can tell it's blood, but that's about it. I wouldn't be surprised if it was her doing though. Actually, I'd bet that it was. That close to here, right after the bombing? And it was fresh."

"So she got them," Sandra said, and nodded to Wallace and Peterson as they headed back in.

"We're going to report on this to the Colonel," Wallace said.

"Not Commander?" Diego asked.

"We decided that title had too much affiliation with Strake," Wallace said. "Nixed it."

"Speaking of Strake," Diego said, a worried expression creasing his face. "Looks like some of his Enforcers broke out."

"What?" Sandra spun on him. "When?"

"While we were gone. Royland told me about it on the way up here. He'd just woken up to prepare for the night, and heard an alarm going off. He's with Karl, and they think Anderson had something to do with it."

"Dammit," Wallace said. "Maybe I should've had his head

instead of just kicking him out."

"You might get your chance," Diego said. "But you better get up there to chat with the Colonel and figure it all out."

Peterson waved a hand, "Just another enemy we'll have to deal with," he said with a sigh.

They left, and Cammie followed them. Sandra and Diego found themselves alone in the pod bay.

He came over and wrapped an arm around her before kissing her on the forehead. "You holding up okay without her?"

"She only just left," Sandra said. She rolled her eyes, but was glad he asked and was even gladder to have his arm around her. "We can keep this place running just fine, I'm sure."

"And she'll be fine," he added.

"You know what's crazy?" She leaned into him, one hand playing with his fingers as she looked out over the rows of police pods. The hanger door was still open, so she was happy to have his warmth against her to counteract the chill wind. "It seems like just yesterday Valerie was basically a pampered vampire princess in training. Within a matter of days, she went from there to defender of New York, a Justice Enforcer appointed by Michael, the vampire of legends. I can't help but worry that it's too much too fast."

"Maybe we should take your mind off of it," Diego said and his lips moved to her neck, his free hand to her hips.

She pushed him away, gently. "Not the right time, Romeo."

"You don't need the distraction?"

"It's more that I'm not exactly in the mood for *that* kind of distraction." She smiled at the way his eyes showed how letdown he was. "Listen, the night is young. But with everything going on, you gotta realize the right times, okay?"

"For you, anything." He smiled and kissed her hand. "As long as you realize that, in the world we live, there might never really be a right time."

She started to chuckle but it stopped, then she frowned. "That's damn depressing."

"Okay, well how's this then?" He pulled her toward the door as he said, "I've been thinking about ways we can pull this city together. We need more than just medical supplies and peace patrols, and a strong city defense for the outside. We need an intel network, Weres and vampires using their enhanced hearing and other senses to work the streets, find out everything we can about the CEOs and where they might have gone, or—"

"Whether they're still operating in the city," she said, getting into it. "Ooh, this is exciting!"

He jumped as she slapped his butt, and she winked.

"I thought you weren't in the mood?" he asked with a smirk.

"You're apparently really good at pushing my buttons. Let's talk more about this, and see where it leads us, if you know what I mean."

He bit his lip and smiled.

Just then, the doors opened and it was Duran, the Were. "Good, there you are."

"What's up?" Sandra asked, trying to hide the smile.

"A blimp from Europe with supplies," Duran said. "Says Strake used to handle all this, and when I came to Cammie, she said to ask you."

"She thinks that because I'm human I'm—"

"Sorry, no, not you." he pointed to her side, "Diego."

"I've been setting up a niche for myself," Diego said with a proud smile. "Figure I could use my head for something too, and numbers have always been kind of my thing. Though I didn't expect this."

"Yeah, so, you got it?" Duran asked.

Diego looked like an idea had just hit him, but he just nodded and said, "Lead the way."

"I'll be in my room," Sandra said, and then added with a playful wink, "Don't take too long."

She hadn't meant for Duran to see it, but he did and said, "Gross, guys. God."

Diego laughed and blew her a kiss, then disappeared with Duran, leaving Sandra to think about all of the possibilities setting up an intel network came with. True to her word, she headed up to her room, and slipped out of her clothes.

To keep herself in the mood, she found some paper and a pen in the desk, then laid on the bed and started sketching out a city map, plotting areas that they hadn't yet spent much time on, or knew to be more dangerous than the others.

When he'd mentioned the idea to her, she doubted he had any idea of the beast he was unleashing. The thought of it made her laugh to herself, and she found herself in a conflicted state of hoping he'd hurry up, and being equally happy if he took as much time as he needed.

She was in her zone.

CHAPTER NINE

The Grave Yard

Valerie's trek through the city made her wonder about the choice of setting off alone. It wasn't that she was worried about her safety by any means, but each time she came across another dark patch where there was no electricity, or a building that looked uninhabitable but had the sound of babies crying, she wanted someone to talk to about it. She needed to make plans, to set up a system where all this would be fixed.

This world had fallen apart somewhere along the way. She didn't know why she felt such an urge to fix it, but more than anything, she wanted to *help* people.

Nobody should have to suffer. Innocent children didn't deserve to die. Men and women should be able to worry about starting a family, not about whether they'd have enough food to avoid starvation.

Somehow, she meant to change all that.

SLOAN AND ANDERLE

But while the CEOs and men and women like them still existed in this world, there could never be peace and joy. Not in the way she envisioned it.

And then there was a whole other level of evil in the world, those like the Duke, the man she called father, because he had created her. He and his plan for world conquest would be met by the legendary vampire, Michael, and be cast down.

She remembered hearing the legends from an elderly priest in Old Paris once, talking to her and her kind before they killed him. He'd said there were once vampires in this world that did good. Told them about religious tales, how the archangel Michael had cast Satan from the heavens.

On that day, he'd told them a dark savior would return, one that would cast them all down, rid the world of their kind, so the pure vampires could rule as they should. To call him a priest was misleading—he'd been a priest of the Nocturnal Order, an old group of vampire worshipers that had risen up after the fall of civilization.

At the time she had thought it was a bunch of bull, but now she wondered. Was she one of these pure vampires now, here for the very purpose he'd spoken of? Or was it all just some big coincidence. She didn't feel 'pure,' by any sense of the word. What she felt was compelled. Compelled by a sense of guilt over what she'd done and witnessed in her past, and by a sense of love for those around her.

Whatever the reasons for her actions, she was damn sure committed to seeing justice return to this world, and ensuring that a sense of Honor be associated with her kind.

A quick look around showed the tall buildings mostly behind her now, what had once been Central Park spread out before her. At the far end, patches of ground glowed a faint green, where she guessed old remnants of chemical waste and who knows what had been dumped, or come to rest, over the years. Far to the west, she could just barely see the outline of Urvant Headquarters, where she and the others had rescued Diego, along with Royland and the rest of the vampires who had been drained of their blood so that the CEOs could stay young.

She walked among withered trees and a field of dirt where she imagined young couples had once walked hand-in-hand for a romantic night stroll, but now had become a place to stash bodies or, if you had money enough to splurge for a headstone, went farther north and made it official.

The Cat's Eye, the hotdog vendor had said.

She considered running back and getting her whole crew out looking for this place, but that would only get people talking. A bunch of badass looking Weres roaming the city might be suspicious. One lady trying to get a drink? Less so.

The park was quiet, almost peaceful if it weren't so damn depressing. The air was cool, still damp from the rain earlier, and she even paused long enough to look up at the stars. Where the clouds had cleared, the stars shone brightly. It wasn't like in the dead cities in the outskirts of Old France, where you could look into the sky and be astounded by the myriad stars gleaming down at you, but here it had its own beauty. Like when the clouds weren't in the way, or the city lights were surrounding you, making the stars harder to see, you'd get a sneak peek and it was rare, so it was majestic.

She wondered if Jackson and Sandra were back at HQ looking at these same stars now, and laughed at herself. Had falling for this guy really made her as corny as that?

No, she realized, remembering nights spent holding Sandra, staring up at the stars together. She had always been appreciative of the world they lived in, curious about what else was out there.

If she'd known then what she knew now, that not only did aliens exist, but were somehow supposedly responsible for who she was now and what she could do, she wondered if she'd have felt differently back then. Maybe more afraid.

It kind of terrified her even more now that she thought about it. Here she was, a woman who could probably take on any challenge thrown her way, but there was intelligent life out there in outer space, possibly ready to wipe them out at any moment.

And Bethany Anne might be out there too, she considered. A comforting thought. If she was out there still defending Earth, and now Michael had returned, there was hope after all. If the two of them ever got together again, maybe with Akio and Yuko at their side, and hell, maybe even Valerie? That would be a force to be reckoned with.

She laughed at the thought of her out there fighting aliens alongside the vampire legends of her youth.

A woman could dream, right?

Something caught her eye and she stopped walking. A shadow moving, and then another. She ducked down, close to the ground to avoid her silhouette being spotted, and ran forward at a crouch. The ground was uneven, hard to see far across, but soon she found a shallow ravine she could duck into.

Focusing her hearing, she heard voices, whispering. No one would be able to hear them, as far as they knew. But they didn't know a vampire was nearby, and probably didn't know vampires had enhanced hearing.

But one thing was for sure—they knew about vampires.

This was clear because she heard one say, "When I get

that vamp blood in me, shit, I'm going over to Elena's and going all night."

"It don't do that," the other voice said in a hiss. "Just makes you younger."

"And helps with healing, I hear. And the way I see it, it probably does so by moving your blood around, rejuvenating it or something, adding extra life to it, which means—"

"Don't say it."

"All night loooong, *baby*." The first voice laughed. "Come on, super vampire blood up in my—"

"I said shut up. This shit's for my dad, as we discussed, right? He's lying on his deathbed, and we can change that, but you're talking about how it's going to help you get your jollies with some chick who can't even stand to look at you? God, shut your trap."

There was a long moment of silence, then a barely audible, "Fuck yourself," followed by a fist to a face, followed by more cursing and the sound of a knife being drawn.

Valerie decided she wasn't going to sit here and let these two jack-holes kill each other before showing her where the bar was. And at this point, she had no doubt they at least had some idea of how to find it.

She jumped up and saw them, thirty yards away one lunging for the other. With a quick sprint she was on them, taking the knife-wielding wrist and snapping it so that it broke and the knife dropped, and then kicking out the other's knee so that they both fell to the ground in agony.

"The hell?!" one shouted.

"The Cat's Eye," she said, pulling her sword and shutting them both up real fast. "I don't care what you two do from here, but you're going to tell me where it is, or your dying dad won't see his son again." She looked between the two,

SLOAN AND ANDERLE

frowning. "I mean, that's noble and all, I get that, but which of you wanted vampire blood to fuel your man stick?"

The one with the broken wrist pointed to the other guy, who was glaring at her in a hate-filled, lustful way.

"You're disgusting," she said, and then kicked him in the face so that his nose cracked and blood went spewing. "Suck up that blood and see what it does for you, jackass." She turned back to the other. "I'm waiting for my answer."

"You… you're crazy."

"Yes, but that doesn't change our situation one bit. In fact, it should make you that much more interested in giving me an answer. NOW!"

He pushed back and up to a kneeling position, cradling his broken wrist. His eyes flitted to the knife on the ground.

"Really?" she said, turning her sword so it caught the moonlight.

He glared, but then nodded and said, "It's our first time. But we were told to follow this ravine until we reached an old bridge, then head due north and there'd be a sign we couldn't miss."

She smiled and said, "See, was that so hard? Oh, and by the way, if I don't find it, I'm going to assume you lied and I'll be back to finish you off. Got it?"

He looked about to argue, so she pushed on her fear powers, causing both to pull back and whimper.

"Good." She gave them a nod and then turned to follow the directions they'd given her.

It was another fifteen minutes or so of walking in the night before she found the bridge. She saw a form approaching and, not wanting anyone to notice her out here, ducked under the bridge. She glanced out and saw a homeless, drugged out looking guy wandering toward the bridge overhead, and decided to wait it out.

She wished she'd just punched him out and kept going, when he stopped above, she heard a zip, and then a stream of steaming urine fell down beside her, way too close for comfort.

Gritting her teeth, she waited, heard him zip up, and then waited for a few more minutes before taking the turn and continuing on her way.

It wasn't long before she saw it, and knew instantly what she was looking at—a large gravestone, set up beside an old, overturned tree, and on the gravestone was a symbol that looked to be sort of religious, but if you turned sideways could clearly be a cat's eye.

If it weren't for her enhanced hearing, she wouldn't have been able to hear the laughing down below. It didn't make sense at first, but she walked to the other side of the large tree and saw the same symbol carved into the bark, and then noticed that what looked like clods of dirt on the upturned roots was moving like a sheet in the wind. She stepped down into the opening and pulled it aside, for it was just that, and it revealed a door with the same symbol.

Smiling to herself, she opened the door and proceeded into a dimly lit staircase that brought her beneath the tree. The bar was a narrow area, not much taller than she, where stools had been set up for the few customers that knew this place existed.

It was quaint in its own way, but the fact that it existed disgusted her. Not even bothering to play games, she said, "You serve vampire blood."

A man built like a tank, with dark skin and piercing eyes, turned to her from behind the bar. He sniffed, and then the white of his eyes showed as they flew wide open.

SLOAN AND ANDERLE

She hadn't even thought to catch his scent, but now that she did, she snarled.

He was a Were.

"We don't need no trouble," the Were told her. "I run my own shop here, and supplies aren't what they once were. Just leave us be and—"

She darted forward, popped him in the throat with the palm of her hand, grabbed his head and then slammed it down on the bar counter. In the aftermath of the violence that erupted, easily holding his head down, she leaned forward to ask him, calmly, "Do I look like I give a damn that your business is slow?"

He choked, trying to regain his breath, as several patrons around them stood, ready to defend him. But when she turned to them with red, glowing eyes and fangs exposed, they all backed off, arms up and and then moved for the door.

"I'm going to ask this once," she said. "*Where* do you get it?"

He looked up at her and snarled, and a moment later he was a bear, practically filling up the whole bar area, bottles cracking.

There wasn't much room for either of them in here, but that didn't worry her.

"Where?" she demanded.

He lunged for her, but she used the tight quarters to her advantage, leaping back and then slapping his paw aside, then darting in to knee him in the gut. She stepped back and kicked his arm so that it was pinned against the wall. Releasing the arm, she kicked off the bar, then the wall as she moved around back and drew her sword, with barely enough room to do so, and held it to his throat.

Valerie hissed, "Another move and you're dead." Sword

pressed hard so there was no doubt whether he felt the blade. "Last chance."

Another roar, and then he was back to his human form, clothes hanging on him in tatters from the transformation.

"I'm not the bad guy," he choked out.

Keeping an eye on him, but stepping back a bit she replied, "Funny, coming from a guy who just transformed into a bear to attack me."

Rubbing his throat he looked sideways at her, "This is my livelihood, there's nothing else!"

She looked him up and down, not like a piece of hunky man-meat, but rather like a new recruit, "You go to Enforcer HQ, ask to speak to Cammie. See if she has something else for you, but you watch yourself or I'll see you return to the graveyard in the way one's meant to be in a graveyard." She paused just a moment, "We could use a bear against the CEOs."

"Your fight's with them?" he looked at her, the fight in his eyes fading. "So's mine." He looked around his empty bar, "Let's talk."

"We can talk after I return to HQ, but right now, you have to earn my trust." She took another step back, but still held the sword at the ready just in case. "So?"

He wiped a line of blood from his neck, then licked it and gave her a curious glance. "You really got a place for me? You really got a battle with the CEOs?"

She stared at him.

He rolled his eyes, "Yeah, yeah, last chance. Gotcha." He went to the bar and took a cup, then poured himself a drink. At her look, he answered, "Don't worry, just beer." He took a long swig, "They ever found out I was the one who told you, I'm going to need an army at my side."

SLOAN AND ANDERLE

She nodded in understanding, "You'll have it."

He returned her nod and set the beer aside, then held himself up with two shaking arms, palms down on the counter. "I've never met one with your strength."

"I'm one of a kind," she said with a smile.

He nodded, then laughed. "Damn, ain't that the truth." He pointed out the back wall, "Keep north. Go to the northern wall, then head west. You'll find a bazaar, sort of like a street market, and if you play your cards right there, you'll find the answers."

"See, was that so hard?" she asked.

He touched the line of blood at his neck again, his eyes glanced at Valerie as he nodded. "Yeah, it kinda was."

"See you at Enforcer HQ, Mr...?"

"Just call me Dreg."

She gave him a nod, and then went on her way, hoping that this next stop would be her last before ending this.

CHAPTER TEN

Enforcer HQ

Cammie glanced back at Enforcer HQ as she walked away, hoping it was in good hands. If Wallace trusted this Donnoly character, then she supposed she could do her best to play along. But the fact that he'd just let Colonel Anderson go, who had then somehow managed to break free a group of the Enforcers, gave her plenty of reason to be wary.

Now she was taking one side of the city, Royland and his vampires the other, with a small contingent of cops staying behind to hold down the fort should anything come up. She had three Weres at her side, including Duran, while other teams had spread out to cover more ground.

With the bombing, and now the breakout, this was more than just a mission to capture the escapees, though. Yes, they hoped to find them, but they also expected to lay down the law on this city and ensure the attackers knew that they weren't going to take any crap.

"Where do we start?" Duran asked, glancing over at two men walking down the street, arm in arm.

"Not by harassing people randomly," Cammie said. "We're here to get this city at ease, and instill a sense of law and discipline. That means with ourselves, too."

"I wasn't implying we go after those two. It's just, who do we even question here?"

"Considering that we've been stuck up in the tower, I figured we'd start by questioning our own." She pointed down one of the main streets, back toward the square where her old bar was. "See if Victor's haunting the old spot, and what he's learned."

"The bar?" the Were to her left said. "Tell me we can grab a drink while we're there."

She laughed, then paused to adjust the heel of her new cowboy boots. That had been one of the first things she'd done after healing up from her scuffle at the Golden City—buy new cowboy boots. Only problem was, the new boots didn't break in as fast as she would've hoped.

"You all right there, boss?" Duran asked with a humorous glance at her boots. "I told you—"

"Oh, shut up." He had gone with her to grab them and warned her about how long they took to break in, but she hadn't cared. She had burned the military outfit she'd worn from her expedition with Diego, hoping the act would erase the memories of being hunted by those other werewolves, and she wasn't about to be caught dead in flats like Valerie wore.

So she sucked it up and ignored the blisters, glad that her Were healing would quickly deal with them. But she couldn't ignore the smirk on Duran's face.

JUDGMENT HAS FALLEN

"Want to keep being an ass, I'll make you walk the rest of the way barefoot." She accentuated the look with a flash of yellow in her eyes, an intimidation that worked well, since most Weres couldn't partially change like she could.

"Hey, I'm just here to help," Duran said. "You wanna ride on my back, or I can carry you like a baby if your feet are hurting. Either way is fine by me."

She glared at him, then continued walking as she said, "Shoes, off. Now."

The other two followed her, but Duran, stood there, head tilted to the side. "I think you're joking, but…?"

"Nope. You're walking barefoot."

"I was offering to help!"

"By saying you could carry me like a fucking baby?" she laughed, then motioned to the other two. "Take his shoes."

"Wait, wait!" he said, hands out defensively as they moved in to follow her orders. "Okay, how about I just buy the first round at the bar?"

"You do realize we're going to ask questions, not get piss-drunk?"

"But the best way to ask questions is with a drink in both parties' hands." His eyes were darting between the other two Weres, who had paused to look back at Cammie. She wasn't sure if the look of hope in their eyes was because they wanted to get the free drinks, or because they wanted to see him walk the whole way barefoot, but she capitulated. "You're sure? Your feet can heal, your coins can never come back."

"I want to buy you all drinks anyway," he said. "My way of saying how happy I am to be on the team."

She assessed him, eyes narrowed, then nodded. "Deal, but one more peep about my boots and you're buying us all steak dinners."

SLOAN AND ANDERLE

His eyes went wide at that, and he mimed zipping his lips. The only steak they got came across on the blimps, part of the trade. As that evening had been the first time they'd seen a trade blimp come through since the fall of Commander Strake, prices had skyrocketed.

Back at HQ, Diego was working out how to trade for medical supplies and more with the captain of the vessel, while Cammie and the others went out on the town to do the dirty work.

The four of them continued walking through the streets, lit up in places with bright lights, eyes piercing dark corners and following anything or anyone who looked mildly suspicious. Whatever Anderson had done with the Enforcers, they didn't seem about to show themselves quite yet.

Cammie was certain there would be a reckoning at some point though, and when there was, she'd be ready.

Soon they came upon the square, where people went about their lives almost as if nothing had happened. Some were clearly uneasy, eyes glancing around as if prepared for an attack to come at any moment, but many were lingering around the fountain telling stories and sharing laughs like they always did, others shopping for food or clothes, and there was the hotdog guy at the edge of the square. Cammie's stomach rumbled and she considered grabbing a hotdog, but there'd be time for that later. Plus, the bar had food, though she'd never liked it as much as those damn dogs.

A cop on patrol nodded their way, and she nodded back, glancing around to see several key spots where cops or vampires were stationed, ready for anything to happen.

If there was a part of the city where people gathered as densely as in Capital Square, she certainly hadn't heard of it. So it stood to reason that, if there was an attack meant to harm people, this would be the spot.

Her eyes cautiously roamed across the crowd, but didn't spot anything suspicious. When they reached the other side and found the alley with the green door, she glanced back one more time and then entered, at relative ease.

A familiar scent of cooking meat and stale beer filled her nostrils and she breathed it in, then let it out with a sigh of relief.

This place felt like home.

"Grab those drinks," she told Duran, and then glanced around for faces she recognized. There weren't many, just a couple of regulars from the old days. Then she saw him. Victor, sitting in the back corner with his eyes on her. He was a large Were, larger than most, and his wide shoulders seemed to take up the whole corner when he stood up from his table to wave her over.

"What brings you here?" Victor asked, giving her a quick hug before they took their seats.

"Can't a woman visit her old haunt and her favorite Were?" She nodded at Duran as he placed two beers on the table, then went back to get more.

Victor followed him with his eyes before looking over to Cammie. "You got him working bitch-boy now?" His face broke into a playful smile.

She shrugged. "Witty banter. How nice that you have time for such simple pleasures."

He frowned. "What's happened?"

"Valerie is separating herself from Enforcer HQ, at least in the public eye, and has gone out looking for trouble."

"A city like this?" He laughed. "She won't have to look far."

She nodded, then took a swig from her beer. She let out

a slow, "Ahhh," and then smiled. "Best beer in all the world, right here."

"Why do you think it's become my base of operations?"

"Yeah, well, maybe I'll have you switch with me and lock you up in Enforcer HQ all day."

He scoffed. "Talk about torture."

"Yeah, well, since we're on the topic of tortu…"

"Who?"

"We lost one of the cops, and he took some former Enforcers with him. If I catch that piece of beetle dung, I'll tear off each of his legs, all three of 'em. So I'm out here, asking politely. Have you seen anything?"

Victor squirmed in his seat with a look of unease. "Remind me never to get on your bad side." He turned and motioned to a Were standing at the back door. "Go spread the word, some former Enforcers are in hiding. We want them. Now."

The Were nodded, then quickly stepped out the back door and closed it. Victor turned back to Cammie.

"So where's that put us?" he asked. "We have this new threat, plus the CEOs and whatever they're up to, some leftover stragglers from that vampire brother of Valerie's, Ella and whatever underground movement there is that's been whining about Valerie moving in and taking over, and… some Nosferatu possibly still in the city."

"You think so?"

"I know so, because we killed a couple last night. I was hoping you'd come by, actually." He leaned in, lowering his voice. "An attack on the west side. Some of my boys were hit last night."

"Anyone killed?"

He shook his head. "That's why I didn't come to you.

JUDGMENT HAS FALLEN

They'll heal, and we can root them out, figure out who did it. But since you're here, I thought you should know."

Cammie made a face, "I would say this city's falling apart, but it never really had it together, did it?"

He laughed a throaty laugh. "No, it did not."

She looked over her shoulder to see that Duran and the other two had joined in conversation with some of the other Weres and, judging by their expressions, were getting similar news.

She turned back to Victor, "Tell me about the attack," she said.

"They were on patrol and were ambushed. First, an explosion, then… they said they were still recovering when a group attacked, guns and all, along with Nosferatu and at least one powerful vampire."

"Shit, what a time for Valerie to run off."

"If she's taken to the streets, she might've already dealt with this." Victor smiled like a giddy schoolboy. "But we can do our part."

This time, she looked at him, a hint of humor in her eyes, "You have something in mind, spit it out."

"We captured one of the attackers, and guess where he is right now."

Her eyes went wide and darted to the room by the back door. That same room she'd beat up Diego when they first met, and where she'd done more than her fair share of beatings before that.

"I also had this little present made for you, though I didn't expect to see you so soon." He waved to the man at the bar, one of the Weres Cammie recognized, but whose name she'd forgotten.

A moment later, the bartender was at their table with a

box he'd been keeping under the bar, and smiled wide. "This must be her then?"

"Allow me to introduce you to Cammie the Cowgirl, as we like to call her," Victor said.

"Call me that and I'll beat you so ugly you'll look like Victor here," Cammie said with a wink to show the guy she was mostly playing around. "It's a pleasure."

"My little gift," Victor said, motioning for her to open the box.

The bartender set it in front of her and said it was a pleasure to meet her, before heading back to the bar where Duran was waving him down for another round.

"Duran, watch yourself," Cammie said over her shoulder, and then turned back to the box. She gave Victor a skeptical look before slowly removing the top, and then froze. "No. Way." She tossed the top away and reached in, grabbing hold of two beautifully carved kali fighting sticks. She felt their weight, and smiled. "Hidden blade and all?" She asked as she played with them.

"Heard you lost your last pair." Victor shrugged. "Figured you couldn't properly deliver your beatings without them, you being a girl Were and all."

She glanced over and asked, "Want to stand up and see what I'm capable of?"

He held his hands up and bit his lip before saying, "I'll be honest, kinda, but not in the way I think you mean."

She whacked him good across the upper arm, leaving a nice welt in the shape of her new kali stick.

"Huh, at least we know they work," he said, rubbing the spot with a half-smile. "And you're as strong as they say."

"Test me again," she said, daring him.

He shook his head and laughed. "Once is enough, and I

want you to save your strength for what comes next.

"Wait, you want me to do the honors?"

He stood and gestured for her to follow. "Shall we?"

"We shall."

She followed him to the back room, feeling the smooth bamboo of her new weapons in her hands, and smiling. The excitement was already sending tingles up her arms.

He opened the door and she stepped in, loving the sound her cowboy boots made on that hardwood floor, and the look of terror in the man's eyes as he looked up at them.

"Don't I know you?" she asked, placing the edge of one of her kali sticks under his chin and lifting it so she could see him better. "Hot damn, Victor, you've captured yourself one of the faction leaders."

"One of the whats?" Victor asked.

"Just a week ago, Valerie had them all together," Cammie said, pulling back her stick and assessing the man as she talked. "First Jackson's crew attacked, and then the remaining faction leaders tried to get Valerie. A couple escaped, and now, lookie here."

"Well hot damn indeed," Victor said, proudly crossing his arms across his chest.

"Yippy for us," Cammie said, and then brought her two sticks for a one-two strike across the man's left arm, carrying them over for another strike on the man's right arm.

The man grunted, but stared up at her defiantly.

"Oh, I'm just trying out my new toy," Cammie said with a giggle. "Don't mind me."

She brought one of the sticks across the man's skull and he groaned, shook it off, and said, "You have no idea what you're up against."

SLOAN AND ANDERLE

"Is that a tease?" she asked. "I do love challenges, so Mr. …?"

"Call me Grolt," he spat at her. "I want you to know the name of the man who'll kill you."

"Grolt… right. Wait, can you say that again? Did I get it right?"

He opened his mouth to answer, but she whacked him across the face with one of her sticks. "Ooh, this is too much fun. See, you hurt some of my boys, and so for that you've gotta pay. Or, you could just tell us where the rest of you are."

He spat blood this time and stared at her defiantly.

"You're working with a Forsaken?" No answer, so she whacked him again. "And the former Enforcers, with Anderson?" she asked. This time his eyes looked confused, though he still remained silent. "So, at least we know you aren't aware of that little predicament."

She whacked him again.

"Ouch, what was that for?" he shouted, struggling with the ropes around his wrists.

"I'm sorry, did I mislead you into thinking I need a reason?" She laughed, then hit him again. "You're just my little piñata, see, and a girl wants her candy."

She stepped forward with a barrage of hits, until strong arms had to pull her back and she became aware of Victor and Duran yelling for her to stop.

Her breaths were coming heavy, images of those damn wolves from the Golden City attacking her, pinning her down in that little hideout, covered in blood…. and she didn't know when the transition happened, or how she'd let her mind go back there.

When she looked up at Grolt, he was dripping blood, one eye swollen shut, a couple of teeth missing. But he glared back at her, defiantly.

"I—a drink," Cammie said, stumbling from the room and handing the kali sticks to Duran. "Get those cleaned off for me."

She had just plopped down at the bar and waved the bartender over, when the sound of breaking glass pulled her back to her senses, and then the gunfire sounded and everyone was shrieking and dropping to the floor.

"There!" a thin woman said, pointing directly to her. "I told you she was here."

The first thing Cammie saw when she followed the direction the woman was shouting to was a line of Nosferatu—mindless vampires, standing with legs spread and fangs at the ready.

Behind them, a man stepped forward, tall, broad chested, and almost bald but for a line of close-cropped hair running down the middle of his head. He wore a suit and untucked dress shirt, and was panting like he'd just run fast.

"So nice of you to fetch me," he said, then sniffed. "Where's Valerie?"

"You're here for her, you're in for a letdown," Cammie said, pushing herself to her feet and allowing her eyes to change to yellow, her claws to grow from her fingertips. "Just me here today."

The vampire shot the woman an angry glance, but then regained his composure and motioned for the Nosferatu to stay as he walked forward. Behind him, a line of men and women appeared, rifles and pistols in hand, and one said, "There're more cops out there, they'll have heard the noise."

"Let them come," the vampire said. "Let them all come, until they bring Valerie."

"You want to use me as bait?" Cammie said. "That's already been tried, and it didn't work."

"I was thinking more along the lines of motivation." The vampire shot forward. In an instant he was beside Cammie, hand at her throat, lifting her from the ground. "See, the thing with Valerie is she doesn't fall for tricks. But she's a simple girl, and when she hears we've killed one of her own, she'll come for revenge."

Coughing sounded and out of the hallway came Grolt, two armed men carrying him.

"She's mine," Grolt said, then spat out more of the blood that was trickling into his mouth from a cut on his forehead.

The vampire smirked, and then tossed her against the walls so that she hit it hard, then fell in a heap.

Grolt stepped up, grabbing a rifle from one of his buddies, and aimed.

A shot rang out, and Cammie opened her eyes, thinking this was it.

She was dead.

But no, the first thing she saw was the vampire stumbling backward, a hole in the side of his head, and then Grolt was shooting again, filling the vampire with shots. The other humans, too, turned on the vampire and his Nosferatu, and they in turn were attacking the men with guns.

Victor was at Cammie's side, Duran at her other, as they pulled her behind the bar.

"We've gotta transform," Victor said, and began to pull at his shirt.

"Not so fast," came a voice from above, and then Ella was above them, on the counter, with a shotgun aimed down at them.

Duran had already transformed but took a shot to the shoulder as he leaped for her. He took out her legs, then fell to the floor with a grunt while she was knocked back into the tables behind her.

The bar was in chaos, and Cammie just shook her head, thinking about how the same thing had happened last time she'd come here.

She was going to have to stop coming to this place.

More werewolves were transforming and joining in the attack, and soon it was every group for themselves—humans, Weres, and the vampire with his Nosferatu.

Then shots came from outside, and the police were arriving. Cammie took down two Nosferatu as a wolf, then returned to her human form to pull Duran from harm's way. She looked over the bar to see that Royland was in the fight now, squared off against the other vampire, but Ella was about to attack him from the rear, and only Cammie could stop her. She jumped on to the bar and transformed as she leaped, landing with a thud that knocked the wind out of her.

A pistol appeared beside Cammie's head and she rolled aside just in time, but when she looked up, Ella was gone.

Several Nosferatu lay dead on the floor and a flash of fighting was coming from Royland and the vampire, each moving too fast for her to clearly see, and then she was there, moving out to clear a path for the cops to get in. They formed a wall, some with riot gear, and Wallace was there shouting, "Everyone, freeze!"

Another crash sounded, and Royland had the vampire's head slammed into the bottles behind the bar, a piece of broken glass jammed into the vampire's neck and his blood splattering everywhere, while others ran for it, some getting caught by the cops, others shot, and some escaping out through the back.

With a shout of pain, Royland pushed the glass and it bit

through his hand as it also went through the vampire's neck, disconnecting head from body.

And then it was over. The Nosferatu he'd brought were dead, the Weres standing with the police, and the others, the ones who had come with Ella, were all dead. Except, she didn't see any sign of Ella.

"Where's she?" Cammie shouted, standing, holding her loose clothes in place. "Where is Ella?"

They all turned, looking around at the chaos and the dead. But there was no sign of Ella. "Dammit to hell!"

Cammie held her head with two hands, trying to piece together everything that had just happened. There'd obviously been a lookout, in case she returned, who'd ran off and notified the Forsaken vampire—maybe thinking she was Valerie? Or maybe the orders had been to shout if anyone was meeting with the Weres. Either way, she had to stop returning to places they might know she'd been, because who knew how many other traps they were setting.

If they hadn't been in place then, they were now.

Cammie shook her head, let down that she'd allowed this mistake to happen. She walked over and helped Duran to stand and motioned for the police.

"Get him in a pod, and back to HQ to heal up."

"And you?" the cop asked.

She ran her fingers through her blood-caked hair, and looked at Victor. He was seething, pissed he'd been so careless. They thought they'd had the upper hand, but it had all fallen apart.

Royland had taken a clean bar rag and wrapped his wounded hand in it, and approached her side. "We have to act fast," he said. "Get this place cleaned up," he told the cops, "while we work to track down those responsible."

JUDGMENT HAS FALLEN

"You need to heal," Cammie told him.

He pulled a vial of blood from his pocket and downed it before answering. "I'll be fine."

So she motioned to the Weres and said, "You heard him. If you aren't wounded from the fight, come with us. We're going on scent here—Weres, spread out first and see if there are other vampires nearby, Forsaken, the type that would travel with Nosferatu. Vampires, we'll need your eyes for the darkness. We have to find Ella, trace her back to their underground."

"You don't think they're working together then?" Wallace said, stepping forward, eyes hopeful. "I mean, she left because of Valerie, because she couldn't see this city run by a vampire."

"Exactly," Cammie said, and then it hit her what he must be going through. "Did… did you see her?"

He nodded. "She looked at me like I was nobody to her. It's over."

"God, I'm so sorry."

Royland cleared his throat to get their attention. At a glare from Cammie, he said, "Me too, but… our window of opportunity is about to shatter."

"Go," Wallace told the two of them. "I'll see to the wounded."

Cammie nodded. They'd meant to set up an intel network, work the streets while maintaining order, but apparently the streets called for a different sort of beast. If they wanted violence, well, Weres and vampires knew how to speak that language well enough.

With a shout from Cammie, they ran off into the night.

It was time to hunt.

CHAPTER ELEVEN

The North Wall, Old Manhattan

Valerie was following the instructions of Dreg, the Were bear, wondering how he was doing and if she'd actually ever see him again. Good for Dreg if she found this place, bad for him if she didn't. She had gone north to the wall and then headed west, and so far had no idea where this bazaar was that he'd mentioned.

When daylight had come, she realized that just wandering around out here, without a clue as to where this bazaar really was, might not be the best idea in the world. Could she walk forever and never find it?

She snorted. They'd write stories about the great Valerie, the wandering vampire who nobody ever saw again.

She noticed what looked like an old bank, its gate partially closed, and slid inside. In the back and out of the way, in case anyone else happened upon this place, she sat cross-legged and closed her eyes. She had a lot to consider. She didn't think about whether she should do anything, but rather how to do it.

Setting up a strong military was key, but should that be by using her so-called soldiers, as she'd taken to calling them, in the police force? Or should it be a military of Weres and vampires? Maybe they could even start conscripting citizens to stand in defense should the CEOs attack? She didn't know what the answer was, though she knew something needed to be done.

This walk up north, by the wall, was proof enough that you couldn't always just set your mind to doing something and then do it. The result could be walking around for a day or two, or forever, without a clue as to where you were actually going.

Well, that wasn't fair, she had a clue. Go west.

She almost laughed out loud at that.

If she made it back to Enforcer HQ and that Were bear was there, she'd be sure to flick him good in the ear for not giving her better instructions.

With her eyes closed, she willed herself to focus on the positive energy. Breathe out the bad, breathe in the good.

Over and over, one breath after another.

Jackson was still alive, and very much into her. That was a positive. Even if she was pushing him away for his own safety, and the safety of the city. Sandra was coming into her own, taking small leadership roles at HQ, and she and Diego seemed exceedingly happy together.

What else could she ask for her best friend?

And the world was a better place, now that Donovan was gone.

She breathed out, then relaxed. It was all wrong, she realized, this way of thinking. Focusing on the past only made her think of the 'yeah, buts.' Instead, she should be thinking of the future.

No matter what happened here today, or the next day, or the day after that, she was going to put this city right. Not just this city, all of America, if she had her way.

Her friends would live long, healthy lives, and the world would be a place without suffering, without hardship.

Again, she almost laughed. If anyone were watching her, she imagined they'd think her ridiculous—sitting there cross-legged, with that silly smirk on her face. She couldn't help it though, because the idea of the world being saved by vampires was just too hilarious.

Everyone else thought they were creatures of the night, evil beings hell-bent on sucking the blood of humans until none remained.

How far from the truth that was.

And the whole alien thing? Since she didn't have the faintest idea what that was about or what it really meant, she decided that keeping that in the 'ignore for a long time' box was a splendid decision.

Her head nodded forward and she caught herself, blinking her eyes to try to stay awake. When had she last slept? She had been sleeping less and less since receiving Michael's blood, and wondered if that was normal, or if she was pushing the boundaries.

Since she wasn't any closer to finding her answers at the moment, however, she decided she wouldn't fight it. If her body was saying it was time for sleep, so be it.

The morning rays of light shone through the bottom of the half-closed gate, casting a golden glow across the floor, but it stopped just short of her. A smile spread across her lips as she watched the little balls of dust dance in the morning

JUDGMENT HAS FALLEN

light, so glad that she didn't have to be afraid of that light ever again.

With her coat balled up as a pillow, she put her sword next to her hand, and laid her head down.

Perhaps answers would come in her sleep.

❖ ❖ ❖

Enforcer HQ

Sandra was sitting in the conference room, or what she had begun terming "The War Room," with Diego, Wallace, and Colonel Donnoly, listening while Wallace briefed them on the previous night's action.

To think that he'd been there amongst the Weres and vampires fighting, but also that Ella and her group had shown up for the fight, was all a bit overwhelming. Add to that the fact that he had a history with Ella, and was somehow briefing them without bursting into tears.

"You're a strong, courageous man," she said, nodding to him when he'd finished.

He and Donnoly stared at her, and Diego shook his head.

"What?" she looked around at them. "Did I say something weird?"

"Just, dear…" Diego put a hand on hers. "As comforting as Wallace might have found that from you, it's not exactly the right thing to say at a police briefing."

"Or in *The War Room*," Donnoly added, gesturing to their surroundings. "But, yes, Wallace, you are everything she said. Do you need a hug?"

Wallace rolled his eyes and said, "I'm glad you can mock me at a time like this. It's nice to be reminded that the only person in the room with a heart is Sandra."

"I—I'm sorry," Diego said. "It's just, you gotta admit, that was a bit girly of her."

"And maybe you all should try being more girly from time to time then," Sandra said, defensively.

Wallace couldn't hide his smile at that, and then even Donnoly laughed.

"Okay, now that that's settled," Sandra said, happy to move on, "what do we do about this whole Cammie and Royland on the prowl thing?"

They looked at her, confused.

"I mean, we have Weres and vampires in the city, but before they were somewhat in hiding. Now it's like a swarm of bees out for blood out there."

"Do bees go for blood?" Diego asked.

"Can we focus on the task at hand and not my crappy metaphors?" she said in almost a growl.

"I'm not sure there is much we can do," Donnoly said. "I have my men on it, doing their best to help while also creating stories to cover what's going on. It's not tough, since it's also true—there's an underground terrorist cell, and we're trying to flush them out."

"And while the hunt goes on?" Sandra asked again. "We can't just sit here sitting on our thumbs."

"As great as that would feel, you're right," Diego said with a wink. "That's why," he paused, looking to Donnoly for confirmation, and then went on, "I've got something to show you."

She wasn't sure what he meant, but the sparkle in his eye told her enough. "Diego, I'm not in the mood for a date right now, this isn't the time."

"It might be the perfect time," Donnoly said. "When we

find something, or the enemy shows their heads, it'll be time for action. For now, it might be best to rest, relax, and spend some quality time with your loved ones."

They blushed, and he quickly added, "Oh, I wasn't implying that you two, well, you know… the big L…"

"Sir," Diego held up his hands like he was praying, "please, just stop."

"Er, yes. What I meant to say is, my wife is bringing the kids over, and I mean to have a bit of my own quality time with them. In times like these, we can't pretend like our lives have already stopped. We can't do that to people we love. Or like a lot. Or… lust after?"

Sandra bit her lip and then laughed. "Oh my God, let's just, yeah. Let's say like a lot." Diego glanced over and she took his hand, adding, "A whole hell of a lot."

"Agreed," Diego said.

"Well, I'd say *The War Room* has been put to good use then," Donnoly said with a laugh. "Everyone, on standby until further notice. Dismissed."

He stood and was the first to leave the room.

"A bit eager, huh?" Diego said. He stood and held out a hand for her. "But I get it, come on."

"Where are you taking me?" she asked, but took his hand and was already getting pulled away.

"You'll see soon enough," he said, and at the elevator he pressed up.

"If you're just taking me to the room to show me your special friend again—"

"No, nothing like that," he said, laughing. "Special friend," he shook his head. "That was funny though."

"Not especially."

He shrugged as the elevator doors opened, and then

SLOAN AND ANDERLE

pulled her in and pressed the button for the roof. "I'm not saying he won't come out to play later, if you play your cards right. Just that isn't the point of this little excursion."

"Well we'll just see then," she said, taking his arm in hers. "I can't imagine what you'd be taking me to the roof for though. We already missed the sunrise thanks to your new-found love of sleeping in."

The elevator dinged and let them out one floor below the roof, so that they had to take the stairs the last bit. When he opened up the doors for her, she didn't see anything special at first, but when he pulled her around to the other side of the roof, she gasped.

"Our guys out at Strake's old fortress found some money," he said. "So… I figured some of it could be put toward good use."

Wooden boxes were set up with dirt inside, and metal arches were in the dirt, rising up so that they were high enough to stand under. He'd even set up little white benches under the arches, and put up a couple of signs that said, "Grapes."

"You planted grapes?" she asked.

"Well, okay, not yet." He blushed, but then went over and gestured. "But right here, I'm going to plant white, and over there, red. The captain of the blimp, he said he can make it happen, no problem. So I put out several orders, figuring it won't hurt to have extras in case pirates intervene or whatever. And when he gets back, I'm growing you a vineyard, specifically for making wine."

"You remembered," she said, amazed, looking at the arches and white benches and back to him. "I mean, I knew you were listening, but I didn't know you were actually *listening*."

"Are you kidding?" He put his arms around her neck and

kissed her, and she kissed him back, passionately. "I'd do anything to make you happy."

Looking at him smiling at her, the sun highlighting his olive skin and the joy in his eyes, she pressed herself against his body and went in for another kiss, then nibbled on his ear as she whispered, "Maybe it's time for that special friend to come play."

He laughed, and kissed her back, but was too excited as he said, "But there's more!"

"More?"

"I might have had some of the guys go find us a corner of a building to rent, where we can set up with a cheese shop and get a wine press going. They said they think they can find the machinery in some of these old factories, and…" He stopped, narrowed his eyes in confusion and pulled back to get a better view of her face, "Are you crying?"

She hadn't realized it, but now that he mentioned it, she wiped a tear away and then hit him. "Why are you so amazing?"

"Maybe I more than just *super* like you?"

"Shut up. You barely know me."

He shrugged and his voice went just a little hoarse. "So, doesn't change how I feel."

She leaned in, head on his shoulder, arms around him and pulling him tight as if the wind could blow him away. "Well I more than super like you too."

"So we're doing it?" he asked.

She pulled back, feeling the beat of her heart quicken. "Oh my god, of course. I mean, to bring wine here, and cheese? I mean, we have to focus on the little things like medical supplies and homes for everyone and all that, and, Ahhh! I can do it all, I know I can."

SLOAN AND ANDERLE

He laughed. "I know you can too… but I was referring to the other thing."

She hit him, and then bit her lip and smiled. She pulled him over to the bench and sat him down, then straddled him. At the moment, she was way too excited to wait for the elevator, and it wasn't like there was anyone else up here anyway.

When you are on the top of the highest building anywhere nearby, it is privacy at it's finest.

Especially if the Were you are with would hear anyone who might be coming up to spoil the fun.

CHAPTER TWELVE

Northern Old Manhattan, Along the Wall

Valerie woke with a start, glancing around to find she was still in the bank.

It was silent. Completely still, without even the sound of the metros or the dull whirr of police pods flying about. How weird it was, such a drastic change only a day's walk away from the heart of the city.

The sunlight was gone, replaced with an almost purple red, and she figured it must be sunset outside.

With a quick look around to make sure no one was with her, sitting silently in the dark, all creepy like—as she often felt people would be doing—she stood, put on her jacket and strapped on her sword, and then stretched with a big yawn. The action reminded her of Diego, when he was in puma form, and she hoped he and Sandra were doing okay.

She envied those two in that they were able to be together without worrying about what the city would think. Just being

SLOAN AND ANDERLE

friends with her put them in danger, sure, but being with each other helped them be that much safer.

The gate was lower than she remembered, or maybe she was just feeling stiff from sleeping on the bank floor, but either way she had to strain herself to go under it. With another yawn, she again set off, heading toward the setting sun in the west.

Soon it was dark, and again she was feeling like this journey was a waste of energy and time.

She almost wanted to turn around and just say screw this. How hard would it be to head out into the Fallen Lands with all of her crew and just go on a rampage until she found the CEOs?

Pretty damn hard, she thought as she considered it. Add skirmishes with other groups, nomads, and whackos and it probably wouldn't be worth it. Even if they were out there, insane or whatever they were, she hated the idea of killing when they didn't deserve it.

So she pushed herself on. She was saving her energy in case she'd need it when she reached the place, but the walk was taking longer than she had expected.

Out here, much of the city was in ruins and dark. She wasn't sure if it was that way because there were no people, or if electricity just didn't reach this far.

At one spot she paused, listening to bottles clank in the darkness, and when she went to investigate she spotted a group of teens gathered around a fire. While they could have been trouble, the longer she listened in to their conversation, the more she was sure they were just some stupid teens out being rebellious.

If they had any idea what sort of monsters might come across them out here, she was sure they would never dare.

JUDGMENT HAS FALLEN

"You kidding?" one of the boys was saying. "I could totally make it across the fire."

She frowned as he undid his pants, pulled it out, and tried to piss from where he stood to the other side of the fire. It hissed pitifully in the fire, and never made it farther than that.

"Gross," one of the girls said. "Put that little thing away before it gets burned."

"Shut up, skank," he said, but did as she asked.

Valerie was about to move on, when the guy backhanded the girl and called her another name, one that Valerie had never heard before, but was pretty sure wasn't good. The others stood and started yelling at him, but he stepped forward to hit her again, and the others weren't moving in to stop him.

With a sigh and a roll of her eyes, Valerie stepped out of hiding and said, "Enough."

The boy turned to her with a crazed look in his eyes, and she knew he'd had a bit more to influence him that night than the bottle of beer in his hand.

"Enforcers are gone," he said, flipping her off. "Since that means you ain't one, and you ain't my mom, go to hell."

Valerie shook her head and kept walking toward them. "Are you okay?" she asked the girl.

With the distraction, the girl was standing, holding her cheek. She shrugged.

The others stared at Valerie, some with anger, some worry.

"Why didn't any of you step in when he hit her?" Valerie asked.

No one said anything, so the guy laughed and said, "Because they know their place around me."

SLOAN AND ANDERLE

"That so?"

He turned from her and said, "Get lost, bitch."

"Apologize to the girl first," Valerie said. "And then to me. You need to learn some respect."

"Her?" The boy stepped up to the girl and grabbed her by the hair. "Hmm, I think I have a better idea. I slap you next, and then—"

Valerie considered pushing out with the fear, something she was realizing she could do. More than anything she wanted to slap this boy silly, but she was worried her strength would be too much, or she'd enjoy it and go overboard. She wasn't here to kill or maim teenage idiots like this, but that didn't mean she couldn't teach him a lesson.

So in a flash, she had him up by his leather jacket and shirt, then casually walked to a wall and hung him on one of several rusty rods sticking out of the half-constructed building.

The group gasped as she drew her sword, its long steel, reflecting in the moonlight. The boy's eyes went wide and his pants darkened where he pissed himself.

But that wasn't enough.

She lifted the sword, ignoring their cries, and struck—

The tip of her sword sliced right through his belt, and his pants fell to his ankles so that he hung, there, flailing and completely exposed. The girl had been right—nothing impressive here.

And a perfect lesson in humility.

"Going commando in times like these?" she said with a look of mock pity. "Not smart at all."

The shrieks from a moment before were gone, replaced by stunned silence, only interrupted by the boy as he shouted and struggled to reach the metal rod behind him.

JUDGMENT HAS FALLEN

"Get me down from here!" he yelled.

Valerie turned to the girl and said, "Your call."

The girl looked at her with confusion, then back to the boy, and started laughing. The others joined in, and their laughter continued as Valerie stepped back into the shadows.

"Remember," she said, and they all stopped laughing. "Justice comes in all forms. Learn some respect, or next time you might find yourself facing worse than a bit of embarrassment. Now, say it."

"I'm sorry, I'm sorry!" he yelled. "Please, just get me down from here!"

"Your *friends* can choose to, or not," she said, and then turned and walked away, smiling at the sound of more laughter.

After a bit she started to wonder if she had been too harsh, but then she shrugged and said, "Screw him." Any guy that thinks he needs to show off by hitting a woman deserves far worse than she'd given him, that was for sure. He'd only gotten off easy because he wasn't a real man yet, as all the others had seen.

She walked past more partially constructed, dark buildings, then turned up a hill that had less obstructing it than the other roads. There was a buzz on the wind. When she came to the top, she froze, smiling in disbelief.

There was a tent before her, and what looked like several rows of more tents leading down into a bit of a valley, where flickering candlelight and the murmur of voices told her this was likely the bazaar she'd been searching for.

The cool breeze, brought with it scents of cinnamon, burnt vanilla, and… cherry incense? She breathed in deep, trying to remember where she'd smelled that combination of aromas before. It brought fleeting memories of a life from long ago.

SLOAN AND ANDERLE

Looking down at herself, that purple coat, the sword at her side, she realized that these were becoming her trademarks. If she was hoping to fit in, to go unrecognized, she'd have to rethink her look.

A glance around showed mostly abandoned buildings, several people bundled up and standing around a fire down a side-street, and, when she paused long enough, she was pretty sure she heard the moans of a couple going at it from the opposite direction.

They'd be distracted. Maybe have tossed some clothes aside.

As much as she hated to do it, she needed to go unrecognized here, so she went in that direction, cautious, moving quick and stepping through the shadows. Luckily for her, it was all shadows out here.

As she grew closer, she saw them, off to the side of the street, but very much out in the open. The woman was on top, mostly clothed except for her left breast which was exposed as the man reached up and groped it awkwardly.

Valerie cringed at the sight, thinking that if this was how most people made love, or whatever they wanted to call it, they were living some damn miserable lives.

But she wasn't here to serve on the love making judge panel, she was here to find a new look.

Her first thought was that it wasn't going to work out—they were still clothed, after all. But suddenly the man rolled the woman over and the dynamic completely changed. He pulled off his shirt and tossed it aside then pulled her up and had her against the wall, taking her from behind and pulling her shirt off too.

"Someone will see!" the woman hissed.

"Ain't no one around but hobos and bums," he said. "Let

JUDGMENT HAS FALLEN

'em get a show, bring some joy to their lives."

"You sick fuck," the woman said, but then moaned, getting into it.

Valerie wanted to look away—this was getting a bit much. But she was looking at the man's discarded shirt and noticed it had fallen on a thick coat that she hadn't seen before.

That would do.

As quick as her vampire powers would let her move while staying silent, she darted forward, snagged the coat, and was away before the smell of sex had enough time to bother her too much. Still, she wanted to gag at the thought of those two, but it was almost enough to make her laugh, and a small part of the whole experience made her even think of Jackson.

Not that they'd ever been so animalistic, but still. She missed the warmth of his hand in hers and the gentle press of his lips.

Damn.

She'd told herself this wasn't going to happen. It wasn't like they had exactly called it off or anything, just realized that he and the city would be in danger if they stayed together.

Maybe she could sneak back there at night, like a nighttime crusader with one goal in mind—her holy grail, if she understood the stories correctly. Or his holy grail, she thought to herself with a laugh.

She cut through the alleys and to one of the abandoned buildings, then moved to a back corner and found an old stairwell with an open spot beneath. Most would only see pure darkness here, but with her vampire sight, she could make out what would work well as a bit of a hiding spot.

With a deep sigh, she pushed the thought of Jackson from her mind, for now. She'd go back for him, there was no way she couldn't. Even as a vampire, a woman had needs. Emotional and physical.

So she bit her lip, ignored the tingling that went up her spine, and took off the purple coat she'd come to love. At first she had planned on just stashing it here, but an idea hit her. Instead of taking the risk, she knelt down and kicked out a section of the wall and then, pausing to make sure no one had heard that, put the old jacket inside the wall.

Next she drew her sword and undid the belt that held it, and stashed them inside the wall as well. Bending over like this, her breasts that, yes, had definitely grown since Michael had given her his blood, pressed against her arms in a way that brought back thoughts of Jackson.

"Dammit," she muttered to herself. "Pull yourself together."

Replacing the section of the wall as best she could, but satisfied it would stay hidden in the darkness, she moved her pistol from her hip to the back of her pants, and put on the man's jacket. Although she'd stolen the jacket, she meant to give it back when this was all over.

Part of her nagged about justice and how it wasn't right, but she was pretty sure there had to be something wrong with having sex in public spaces, so could justify that lending his coat to her for a bit was punishment.

Justice wasn't law.

It was a stretch, but she went with it. How else would she get around out there without risking the possibility of being recognized?

The coat was a thick one. Brown with pockets at the chest and a hood lined with what had to be fake fur. She pulled up the hood, glad to have this extra bit of concealment, and then headed back outside.

JUDGMENT HAS FALLEN

When she'd left the building, she heard the sound of a woman squealing, then calling out way louder than was appropriate. The homeless people by the fire were running over to see what was happening, and Valerie had to laugh at the idea of them all stumbling across the couple.

The noises also meant they were probably about done, so she needed to get moving before the man started looking for his coat. The one walking off into the distance.

Turning to the tents of the bazaar, she descended the hill, hands in pocket, hood up.

When she entered the first tent, a man stood at two flaps at the rear, arms crossed, glaring. He tilted his head her way, and she stood there, unsure what to do, as music wafted out from behind him. Laughter, and then someone came stumbling out, obviously drunk and gave her a wary look before disappearing into the night.

Valerie glanced back then to the man standing guard, and said, "I'm here."

"What?"

"One of the dancers." She was taking a bit of a leap here, but based on the look in the eyes of the man who had just crept past her, and the music, she figured it wasn't too far off.

The man looked at her with doubt, so she unzipped the jacket to show off. Her sleeveless blouse, two sizes too small now at the chest, did a pretty damn good job of convincing him.

He smiled and the look of lust came over him, but then suspicion returned. "You're not supposed to be out here. What're you doing?"

Pursing her lips, she shrugged and nodded back toward the darkness. "One of the customers wanted a, er, *word*."

"Shit, keep that between you and Clive," the man said,

and then held open one of the tent flaps. "Best get in there before he has your ass cut up."

Those words caught her off-guard, but she put on her best smile and tried to look both apologetic and afraid as she walked past. As soon as she was in, she pulled the coat back tight around her and stood tall.

How was this place still existing? She'd thought her people were cleaning up, but if this was still within the city walls, she imagined there was a lot more to discover in the city, but one step at a time.

The first couple of tents were tied together in a way that made one big one, with several men and women lingering with drinks, or each other, in hand. They'd look up at her, but just keep making out or wallowing in drunken self-pity.

Then she found herself by some stairs at the edge of a large tarp, leading down to what must have once been a construction site hollowed out but never built up, she guessed by the cement blocks poured into the ground at the base of the stairs. When she reached the bottom, there was an actual door with plaster on each side—a wall with the tent flaps attached.

It was starting to remind her of the old stories she'd heard about haunted houses. With a 'here goes nothing' attitude, she pushed through the door and stood still staring at the sight.

Before her was a whole market of tables selling food, spices, weapons, and more. Crowds of people, from the apparently homeless to the much better off, walked about shopping, or staring longingly at the goods for sale. Down here, it felt like they were all equal in the excitement of the market.

She stepped forward and looked up at the tarp ceiling, rippling in the night wind, but lined with beams and rows of bright orange lights that gave the whole place an eerie glow. Some of the tables around her also had torches burning, so shadows flickered across the faces of the passersby.

"Care to sample our fruits?" a man with thick, white eyebrows said, holding out a plate of dates. "Just arrived with last week's dirigibles, you can't get finer."

With a shake of her head, she continued, and soon learned it was easier to just ignore all the merchants. More than once the crowds almost knocked her over, and when one tall woman bumped shoulders with her, she was ready to pounce. It was all overwhelming, and she would've loved to have Jackson or Sandra here with her.

The tall woman looked at her like she was crazy, and said, "Watch it, man," before continuing on.

Valerie considered those words, and then wondered. With the thick coat on and her hood pulled up, could she pass for a man down here? The lighting was dark, and with it being so crowded, they probably couldn't make out her tight jeans—she'd even seen a couple of men wearing pants as tight as these, so that might not be a consideration.

She decided to test it out, and at the next table, one selling everything from toilet paper to rolls of gauze, she paused, looking down at the goods.

"How can I help you, sir?" the plump woman behind the table asked. Valerie looked up with a smile, and the woman cringed. "Er, ma'am. My apologies."

"Think nothing of it," Valerie replied. "I chose to wear my husband's coat, after all."

The woman blushed, but nodded at the goods. "Is there something I can help you find?"

Valerie looked at the gauze, then noticed a table behind the woman, where underneath it were boxes with the old symbol of medicine—two snakes wrapped around a stick or whatever that was.

"Where does all this come from?" she asked.

"I have my suppliers," the woman said, eyeing her suspiciously. "Who's asking?"

Valerie didn't feel like beating around the bush here, so she got to the point. "You do realize there's a whole city out there in need of medical supplies?"

"I think it's time you move on, lady." The woman turned to the next customer over, but Valerie had an idea. She stepped closer, lowering her voice, "And if I had money to pay for the best healing available?"

The woman paused, scratched her chin thoughtfully, and turned back to her. "You're asking questions you shouldn't be asking."

Valerie smiled warmly, and reached into her pocket to hand over a coin—only, she just realized, she'd left her coins and blood vials stashed away with her purple jacket in the abandoned building. *Merde.*

The woman saw what she was doing and waited patiently, but when Valerie didn't pull out any money, her expression soured. Valerie made a note to herself to remember this woman. When Sandra and the others heard about this, they could get a crew of Weres down here to see that the medical supplies were properly distributed to those in need.

With that thought, Valerie glanced around and realized how much other stuff in here could be put to good use.

"Get lost," the woman said.

Another shopper looked at Valerie out of the corner of his eyes, and she noticed. He nodded her over.

"You got other ways of paying," he said, voice low, "we can talk."

JUDGMENT HAS FALLEN

"Is that so?" Her voice was like a purr, playing along.

A plump woman shook her head at Valerie and mouthed, "Run," but Valerie could fend for herself, so she ignored her.

"Follow me," the man said. "Not too close though. We don't want Clive's men getting the wrong idea."

They walked farther into the bazaar, turning down rows of tables that increasingly felt sketchier. Some had bottles of green and orange liquid of a type that Valerie had never seen before, and could only guess was some sort of drug, while others literally had women in skimpy clothing sitting on a back row like bleachers as men pointed at them and haggled with the so-called merchants.

In this area, trailers were parked behind some of the tables, and farther back there were walls set up, separating the main area from a back room with lights flashing.

"You're new here," the man said, more of a statement than a question. "Gotta learn fast that you don't go asking certain questions in public places."

"Thanks for the tip."

"Just here to help." He glanced back and eyed the coat. "You're gonna want to lose that thing though, if you hope to get some of the juice."

"The juice?"

He rolled his eyes and stopped walking long enough for her to catch up, so that when he lowered his voice she could hear him. "The word on the street for what you're seeking. You are seeking it, right? I didn't misunderstand you back there?"

"A red juice, correct?" She watched him as she said it, and his eyes lit up as she mouthed, "Blood."

He glanced around, nervously, "Don't fucking think of saying it, not even mouthing it." He then motioned to an area behind several tables where one of the trailers was parked. "Forget this, I gotta see what we're dealing with here."

"Excuse me?"

He walked toward one of the trailers, not looking back, just motioning for her to follow.

"This better be where you keep it," Valerie said, starting to get annoyed at this guy. She had a bad feeling about him.

"Where I keep it?" He glanced back at her as he reached a trailer door. A man stuck his head out from the other side, but saw the two of them and simply nodded before going back where he came from. "Just get inside."

She sighed, already getting what was happening here. This son of a bitch lured women in here for who knows what. She tilted her head, sighed, and then figured that, what the hell, she might as well find out before deciding what his punishment should be.

He smiled when she walked up the steps of the trailer, then followed her in and shut the door.

It was a weird sensation, knowing you were with some sort of predator but not being scared in the slightest.

The trailer had a dim, blue light in it, the type that made everything feel calm. She imagined it helped the other girls not freak out, but in her case, it just made her mad.

"Come on, off with it," the man said, standing with the door closed. "If we're going to walk in there offering favors for the juice, I gotta know they'll be willing to sell."

"In where, exactly?" she asked, then gestured toward the direction she'd seen the flashing lights. "We're talking about that room? What, that's where the girls dance… maybe more?"

His expression changed to irritation as he glanced at the door behind him. "You think I have all day here?"

JUDGMENT HAS FALLEN

She narrowed her eyes and focused on his thoughts. While she couldn't read minds yet, not like Akio at least, she felt the wave of his emotions flow over her. Irritated, but… not aggressive.

That surprised her.

"You're not going to try anything here?" she asked, more out of confirmation.

"What?" he laughed. "You kidding me? We got Clive out there with his butchers, and Norma in there with her slicers. I walk around here worried I'm gonna get my throat slit one minute, sold off to those predators the next, and you're asking if I'm about to attack you or some shit?" He turned to the door and reached for the handle. "I don't have time for this, get lost."

"Wait," she reached out and touched his shoulder. "I might have misjudged you."

He hesitated, but shook his head. "Lady, you're striking me as more trouble than the money I make from these connections, got it? So if you don't mind."

She hated to do it this way, but revealing her true nature right now didn't seem like the best idea, so instead she stepped back and dropped the coat.

Judging by the way his eyes went wide and his jaw fell open, he was impressed.

"Shit, girl," he bit his lip. "You gonna get yourself a year's supply if you play your cards right. Might even get Norma to take you in as one of her regulars, if you're in for the long haul."

"So you're saying you'll make the introductions?" she asked.

"Yes, I will." He motioned to the coat. "Okay, put that back on so we don't have any competition. We gotta get you

SLOAN AND ANDERLE

to Norma. She pays the best and, honestly, you'll be damn glad I didn't take you to Clive. Guy's a real prick."

"Thanks…?"

"Owen," the guy said.

"Thanks, Owen."

She bent down to grab the jacket and noticed how he blushed when she caught him looking at her cleavage. A real predator wouldn't blush like that, she thought, and smiled as she stood. With a nod of approval, she pulled her jacket on tight and zipped it.

He didn't know how lucky he was that she'd waited to act before simply jumping to her first conclusion.

Would he suffer later for what he was doing in assisting in this whole trade business? Of course, she would see that he did.

However, she had to get to the bottom of it first.

CHAPTER THIRTEEN

Capital Square

Cammie refused to go back to Enforcer HQ until she found something. Anything. Sure, Royland had to go back, or at least find somewhere to hide out during the day, but she had no excuses aside from the need for rest.

Even rest was, in her opinion, overrated. She had stopped by her underground fortress to check in there, grab some beef jerky and an apple, and then went back to the streets.

Instead of hoping to pick up a scent, however, she figured she would try another tactic.

Jackson.

She had found him at the hotdog vendor, the night sky pushed back here by all the bright lights and billboards. He stopped to speak to a crowd of people about how the city was theirs again, and treated them each to a dog, until the vendor was out and had to close shop to go scrounge up some more.

It was cute how he had lingered by a shoe stall, eyes on a

pair of Pumas, just like the ones Valerie wore.

But that didn't change her suspicion. She'd always heard of Jackson Mercer while roaming the streets of this city. He wasn't just some nobody, some summer fling for Valerie and then that was it—he was one of the eight faction leaders. The men and women Strake had always been so worried about keeping in check, too scared to simply do away with because of the power they held.

It was even rumored that they, or their parents before them in some cases, had been around before Strake came to power. Back then they all fought for control of the Eight Points, a part of the city that Strake had quickly taken for his own as a symbolic gesture. There was to be no more fighting.

Well then Valerie came along and did away with Strake, and in the process the faction leaders were in hiding or killed off, all but Jackson Mercer.

How he'd managed to weasel his way into the heart of the most powerful woman—or vampire—in Old New York, Cammie could not possibly fathom.

Sure, he was a good looking dude. And he had power. And, judging by that look at those shoes, he had a bit of a heart to him.

But…

She watched as he led his throng of followers across the square, said his farewells, and then entered a building with a handful of them still in tow.

He was the one man outside of Enforcer HQ with influence left in this city. If he didn't know where Ella was, maybe nobody would. The only problem, of course, was that Valerie would probably punch her in the throat if she found out this was happening. A good ear flicking was fine, but a vampire punch to the throat?

JUDGMENT HAS FALLEN

Not so much.

So, Cammie had to be sneaky.

Moving along the side of the square, she went to the building Jackson had entered and then ran around to the side. Here she found an old door to the kitchen, the type that are in the cellar, and worked her way in. She waited, and then heard footsteps. Following them, she paused at a spot where the hall led into a larger cellar, and then there was a set of stairs that led up. Voices were coming down, and one of them Jackson's.

"It's wearing on me is all," he said. "I'm no politician."

"You have no choice but to be," a female voice said in response. Could it be Ella? Cammie scooted forward, cautious. She was known to jump to conclusions at times, and now was not the best time for that.

"Please tell me it's as late as I think it is, and I'm not getting as old as I feel."

"Sir," the female voice said, and Cammie lost the rest as she backed up, biting her tongue. She'd hoped it was so simple, but no, Ella would never refer to Jackson as 'sir.'

"You hear something?" Jackson said, and the footsteps moved for the stairs.

Cammie glanced around, not wanting to go back the way she came, and noticed a small cut out behind a piece of plywood. Gently moving it aside, she discovered a small passage and decided this was a better hiding spot.

As soon as she'd entered, however, the female voice said, "I'm sure it's nothing."

"Yeah, maybe."

The footsteps walked off and their voices grew muffled, so Cammie was about to continue her eavesdropping, when another noise came, not far off in the passageway she was in.

SLOAN AND ANDERLE

Not sure what to make of it, but certain her curiosity would kill her if she didn't go find out what it was, she allowed her eyes to turn yellow, so that she could better see in the dark.

It was just an empty area under the foundation of the building, and the noise was likely a rat, she figured. But when she was about to turn around, she heard it again, and this time it was accompanied by another—this one definitely a voice.

Who else would be down here? She could think of a couple of answers to that. Ella, for one.

So she went deeper into the skeleton of the foundation until she came upon an area of the ground that was cut out into part of a tunnel. Ducking down to see inside, she saw that it led to the sewers. When she looked up to judge which direction it went she could see that it led farther back along the way that other restaurants and businesses would be.

Following Jackson was easy, but an opportunity like this didn't come along every night.

She gently lowered herself into the tunnel, and soon found herself walking along a metal walkway beside the sewers. The voices grew louder with each step, and soon she could make out one of them asking questions about vampire blood.

"You don't get your money back," a deep guttural voice said.

"No, it's not about that," another replied. "I simply want to know its effects."

"You paid me before knowing what it'd do? That's rich!"

She carefully moved forward, assessing the various offshoots of these tunnels, trying to gauge which direction the voices were coming from. The last thing she wanted to do down here was try to use her nose to catch a whiff of them, what with the sewage smell already hard enough to fight off.

And no matter how quietly she walked down here, the damn metal walkway clanked and rattled, so that, when she reached the third offshoot, one of the voices said, "Someone's here! Get that shit out of my face," and took off running.

The clattering told her which way he was going, but the other guy had stuff, so she headed toward where the noise had started.

She came out in an open area that had multiple levels of these sewage walkways, and saw a man staring down at her wide-eyed from above, a small pack in his hands. If she were a betting woman, she'd have put money on that pack containing a lot of it.

"Stop!" she called and ran out, jumped onto the handrail of her walkway, and then leaped up to grab ahold of the one above, and pulled herself up.

The man's eyes went wide and he turned to run, but she was already on him. The case went flying and vials spilled out, clattering across the walkway before falling into the sewage below. All but one, which she snatched up before turning back to the man.

"Holy fartbags lady," the man said, loosening his tie as he assessed her, trying to figure out how mad he was allowed to be. "You just cost me a year's salary."

"Vampire blood?" she asked, and pulled the stopper to take a whiff. Oh yeah, definitely vampire blood. "Tell me where you got this."

He stood, deciding to be defiant, so she kicked his legs out from under him and leaped onto him, knee in his back.

"WHERE?!"

"The man who just ran, talk to him!" the man said, about to break into tears.

SLOAN AND ANDERLE

"Shit!" She slammed his face into the metal walkway for good measure, and then was up, running in the direction she'd guessed he had gone. She could stay here, trying to get answers out of this man, but judging by the way he was acting like a baby, it was likely time wasted that could be better spent in the right direction.

But she held onto the vial, so that she'd at least have something to show Valerie, if this didn't work out.

Proof that the blood trade was still *very much* alive.

She saw a shadow dart ahead, and pushed herself, leveraging her Were power but not wanting to transform and risk dropping the vial of vampire blood. At the corner she pushed off the wall to get extra momentum and ran, and then saw the man leaping from the walkway to a nearby rock shelf.

Almost there, she let her claws out and allowed her sharp teeth to extend, and leaped for him. They were in some other part of the city now, she was sure of it, and though it was still the sewer, it reminded her of an ancient cave like you would hear explorers brag about.

She snagged his arm.

The man was lanky with hair falling down to his shoulders. He wore a simple T-shirt with the symbol of a knotted tree, and carried a backpack which she figured he used to transport the blood.

She jerked him around, "End of the road," she said. "Time to talk."

"You think you scare me," he said, voice shaking in terror. "There're worse monsters, there's—AHH!"

SMASH!

The ceiling had suddenly dropped down on him, swinging at an angle, and impaling him with three large spikes, before moving back up and leaving his body to simply drop

JUDGMENT HAS FALLEN

dead, and roll off the side into the sewage water below.

Cammie took a step back, mouthing *What the Fu*—when her foot hit a wire and she felt something cinch around her ankle before pulling her up.

No way in hell was this happening, she thought, transforming into a wolf and barely slipping out just as a ceiling plate moved and would have smashed her to bone-meal.

She landed and then lay there, breathing heavy, leg throbbing in pain, and could barely keep her head up as the whole area seemed to pulse. The man was dead, that was for sure. The traps had nearly gotten her too, and for what?

Slowly, she pulled herself together and knelt, assessing her surroundings. There was a patch of metal barely visible in the dirt that covered more of the ground closer to the rock wall. Her Were eyes were just able to pick up the reflection of a distant light on a string, which, when she followed it to the walls, looked like it could either result in an explosion or maybe another wall movement. Above, she saw a metal cage that she'd probably noticed earlier but just thought to be part of the walkway. It was possible that would come down and sweep someone into the sewage, trapping them there until they drowned.

Forget this place, she thought, and turned back the way she had come. Careful where she placed each step, she backtracked and only allowed herself to breathe out loud when she was back on the metal walkway.

Her first instinct was to run from this place and never return.

But then she thought about it. A hidden area with traps like this was definitely protecting something. Ella? The CEOs? A store of vampire blood and the pirates smuggling it?

Whatever it was, she had to make sure she could find her

way back here, and had to bring Valerie. There was no one else she trusted to be able to get past those traps, and if there was a real danger in there, Valerie could handle it.

She turned and began her trek back, cursing with each step noting the droplets of blood that fell from where the wire had gripped her leg. It would heal, but damn she wished her healing was instantaneous.

❖ ❖ ❖

Restaurant in Old Manhattan

Sandra smiled at Lorain, who had an intense look of concentration on her face as she spelled out her name while, nearby, Jackson stood watching approvingly.

"Very well done," Sandra said, smiling. Lorain blushed, but it was clear she was proud.

"Thank you, for this," Jackson said when Sandra stood, preparing to leave. "I know you're busy, so—"

"Nonsense," Sandra said. "She needs to be learning, and I'm happy to do my part. At least the art of reading and writing mustn't be forgotten."

"It's hard to convince families of that nowadays, when they're so worried about simply surviving from one day to the next."

The back door opened and Diego and Wallace entered.

"No sign of her?" Jackson asked, and Wallace shook his head. "And if there were?"

"She's a different woman than the one I had feelings for," Wallace said. "I get that."

"We should get back to HQ." Diego wrapped an arm around Sandra's shoulders. She leaned into him, loving the feeling of an almost normal life. The two had escorted her out here so that she could help tutor Lorain, who could then teach the other teens and kids who had missed out on education in favor of learning to survive.

Sandra, however, had been raised in a privileged class, learning what schools of the old days might've considered important. Now she was happy to see that she could do her part for the city, in addition to just knowing how to use a sniper rifle, her brain was coming in handy.

Plus, on the way back they were planning on stopping by the storefront where she'd be making her wine and cheese, once they got a few more steps figured out.

With a glance back to see that Wallace was on lookout, standing at the door and facing away, she leaned over to get closer to Jackson and asked, "So, Ella?"

He shook his head, and then whispered, "She's so far gone to the other side…"

Sandra shook her head. "Yeah, got it." Poor Wallace. She couldn't imagine what she'd do at this point if Diego suddenly switched sides. He seemed to be thinking the same thing, because he squeezed her gently and then gave her a kiss on the cheek.

Jackson didn't need to ask about Valerie, though his eyes showed the pain of being apart from her. Sandra could understand it, though that didn't mean she had to agree with the decision. Valerie wanted to keep the city safe by setting up Jackson for a leadership position separate from her—he was the city's best bet, at this point. A council of leaders, with him, Donnoly for the police, and so on, while Valerie cleaned up the trash and did her best to cut any ties to the CEOs.

What if they attacked right now, though, Sandra wondered? Would she and the others be enough to defend the city?

SLOAN AND ANDERLE

Wallace cleared his throat, looking back at them from the doorway.

"Coming," Sandra said, and gave Diego a quick squeeze, and then walked back over to Lorain. "You keep practicing, you're a smart girl. We'll get into math next time, maybe try some French even."

"I'd like that," Lorain said. "It's been nice being able to defend myself with the training Jackson insisted we all receive, but something about this type of learning makes me forget all the problems we face."

"If we can give that feeling to a good portion of the children and teens of this city?" Sandra said, "I think we can consider this a success."

"Agreed." Lorain smiled and then hugged Sandra. Caught off guard, Sandra smiled and hugged her back. "Tomorrow?"

"Of course," Sandra agreed.

She went back and took Diego's hand, and the two followed Wallace outside, stopping briefly to wave to Jackson.

"Sure you don't want to come see the place?" Sandra asked.

Jackson sighed. "Got my top people coming by to discuss how to deal with... all this."

"You can say it," Wallace said. "I'm heartbroken, not stupid. Ella has gone over to the other side."

Jackson nodded. "You're a wise man, Wallace."

Wallace scoffed.

They had just turned to go when a grating at the side of the street clanked, and then moved out of place.

"What the...?" Wallace said, hand on his pistol as he stepped toward the grate.

Sandra pulled back, allowing Diego to step in between her and the grate. And then, to their surprise, Cammie came climbing out.

JUDGMENT HAS FALLEN

"The hell are you doing in the sewers?" Diego asked.

"Nearly getting killed," she said, motioning to the hurt leg and tears in her clothes. "You just going to stand there gawking, or do you want to help me?"

Wallace stepped forward, helping her to stand, and they turned to notice Jackson and Lorain in the doorway.

"Cammie, that you?" Jackson asked. "Shit, you okay? And I use that word literally, because you smell like shit."

She rolled her eyes, "You still have a crappy sense of humor," she retorted.

He shrugged with a half smile. "But seriously, what happened?"

"Long story. Is Valerie back yet?"

"Haven't seen her," Sandra said.

"Yeah, well," Cammie glanced around to ensure no one else was around, "suffice it to say that the blood trade is still in effect."

Sandra thought she noticed a quick, suspicious glance Jackson's way, but realized she might have imagined it.

"Well, Valerie trusted us to manage the city," Sandra said. "Let's regroup at HQ, form up teams, and get to work on those bastards. How about you, Jackson?"

"My people are trying to root out the resistance fighters, who we've received word are calling themselves 'The Stake.'"

"The *Stake*?"

"I suppose it's a play on Strake, but also the fact that, in legend, stakes were used to kill vampires." Jackson shook his head. "It's not great, but their mission is one of violence, not creativity."

Sandra sighed and looked back at Enforcer HQ, wondering how she had gone from a youth of fearing so called creatures of the night, to now standing at their defense. There was

SLOAN AND ANDERLE

one reason—Valerie. And right now, she sure was missing her.

But they could do this, or damn well do their best.

CHAPTER FOURTEEN

The Bazaar

Valerie followed Owen back out through the trailers and increasingly dark parts of the stalls where vendors were selling knives and guns, sex, anything that would make normal people uncomfortable.

They just made Valerie want to punch everyone. A punch for you, a punch for Owen, and two-double punches for the guy with the orange shirt. That color could blind someone.

She was here with a goal though, and that was finding those behind the blood trade, or any connection she could find to the CEOs. She'd start here, and maybe then get started on cleaning up the streets, including this riff-raff.

A couple of the girls eyed her as she walked by, but she stayed focused on the room with the bright lights and loud music ahead.

"Might want to lose the coat before we go inside," Owen said. "It's not exactly helping to sell your best features."

SLOAN AND ANDERLE

She glanced at him with a raised eyebrow and started undoing the coat, but then noticed a man walking along, two aisles over, glancing her way while trying to appear as if he wasn't.

"I think I'll wait until we're closer," she said.

Owen saw where she was looking and nodded, pulling her along with a hand on the small of her back. She debated breaking that hand, but knew that doing so wouldn't help in her mission any.

"That one's trouble," he said, lowering his voice and trying not to look. "Not sure what he wants with you, but if you've got his attention, best proceed with caution."

"I'm not too worried."

"No?" Owen shook his head. "I wonder if the two women found dead were worried or not. Yeah, that's right. Everyone saw them leaving with him, saw his hands all over where they shouldn't be, and then… he comes walking back in here not half an hour later, alone. When they found the bodies outside, no one said anything, but they all knew."

"The police aren't exactly our best friends down here," she said nonchalantly, trying to get his take on where the authorities stood.

He looked over with a frown, then made a tsking sound with his tongue. "Don't even say that word around here. You gotta be new. Shii—it."

"Caught me." She did a double step to keep up as they made a turn. A quick glance showed the sketchy guy was still tailing them. "So… who does take care of business down here?"

"Like I said, Clive has his butchers, Norma her slicers. But homeboy there rides in Clive's circles, so he won't touch him. You rat him out to Norma, she'd likely prefer not to start a war, even if the girls that he got to were hers."

Valerie shook her head, processing all this. Taking care of one aspect of the city had opened her eyes to various other issues. All of this on top of the blood trade? She hadn't even asked around about the pirates, such as the ones who had taken down the blimp she'd ridden over from Europe. With a sigh, she realized it was just one issue after another here.

First things first, though.

"You can leave the coat there," Owen said, pointing to a series of hooks along the outside wall.

She was about to, when she remembered the pistol stuck into the back of her pants. While before she'd been able to keep Owen from noticing it because she was in that small trailer with her back to the wall, now she'd be going into this club, showing off the goods in hopes that doing so would get her close to her target.

The ground was dirt over here, so she got an idea. As she let the coat fall from her shoulders, she pretended not to be able to catch it. She dropped to one knee to grab the coat, and in one quick move set the pistol against the wall and brushed dirt across it. Not perfect, but she'd made enough of a mound to cover it while appearing almost natural.

She stood and smiled, hanging the coat on one of the hooks. "Silly me, always so clumsy."

He sighed and shook his head. "Graceful and sexy from now on, got it?" with another glance back, he said, "Your friend's gone at least."

She wasn't so sure, but nodded and followed Owen to the doors.

Three large men stood with pistols holstered, shifty eyes looking for a reason to use them. They glanced at Owen and then at her, then stepped out of the way. Walking past them, she had to remind herself that she was a badass vampire who had taken on way worse than them. When they stepped back into the cover of the doorway, she felt like she'd just been barricaded in by massive gates.

The lights flashed in hues of blue and red, people dancing, throwing themselves around like the world had never collapsed and there wasn't an army of mercenaries out there waiting to take down the city.

She almost envied them their ability to get lost in their movements, and paused to watch as the throng swayed with the music. Each beat sent vibrations through her, the scent of sweat and perfume almost beating out the cigarette smoke.

And then another smell hit her—vampire.

Her eyes searched the crowd, but there were too many of them for her to hone in on who was a Forsaken. Then it was gone, and she wondered if she had imagined it. But no, she was quite sure of her senses, and as she followed Owen up a set of stairs to the left, she kept her eyes on the crowd below.

"Through here," he said, leading them to one of the many curtained off side-rooms.

She hesitated. Not because she was scared by any means, but because she wanted to turn and find the Forsaken in the crowd. Going undercover meant she had to stick with the story for now, so she smiled and slipped under the curtain.

He followed, and they were in a half-moon shaped room with candelabras lining the walls above plush couches. At one end sat a slender woman with dark skin, her hair combed to one side to frame her face and accentuate her high cheekbones.

Owen cleared his throat and nodded for Valerie to approach, then said under his breath, "Go on, show yourself off."

JUDGMENT HAS FALLEN

She wanted to kick his smug grin off his face, but stepped forward and did as she was told. As she spun, she noted the pistols holstered on the men standing behind the couches, lingering in the darkness.

"What is this?" the lady said, but her eyes showed she was intrigued.

"A new one for your treasure trove, Norma." Owen stood tall, thumbs in his belt loops. "A volunteer."

"Red light or black?"

Owen's expression changed to one of uncertainty, and then he said, "I imagine she'd perform well in either, mistress."

The word mistress sent a chill up Valerie's spine as she thought about all those times Sandra had referred to her so. She hoped they were doing better than this. Right away Valerie could tell this woman was not a Were or Forsaken, and although her thoughts pulsed with manipulation, she had a feeling getting close to Clive would be the best way to go here.

Taking a gamble based on the fact that she knew the term red light districts from Old France, she said, "I'll go for black."

"She knows how to speak for herself then?" Norma said, less than impressed with this fact. "But can she fight?"

Ah, so black had to do with fighting. Valerie stood tall and smiled. "Try me."

Norma glared, reached onto the table before her for what looked like an orange mint, but it could have been anything, and then plopped it into her mouth. Sucking on the mint, she assessed Valerie, and then snapped her fingers.

One of the men took off his jacket and pistol, setting them aside so that he could approach Valerie.

Was this actually happening? She wanted to laugh. She had to remind herself to take it easy. Her goal here was to

SLOAN AND ANDERLE

be one with the shadow world, uncover its secrets, and then undo it so that the city could go on in peace. It wouldn't help anyone to destroy this guy and reveal what she was.

The first punch was fast, and she let it barely connect so that it looked like she was fast at dodging, but not too fast.

"How far does this go?" she asked as another punch came and she dodged underneath.

"For now, just a demonstration. The real fight will come soon enough."

Valerie nodded, then let the guy get a punch to her stomach. She doubled over, pretending it bothered her, and then came up with a short uppercut and a sweep of her legs—enough to knock him backward and then send him to the ground.

With a pounce she was on him, one hand on his throat, another lifted to deliver a strike. But instead of hitting, she looked up to Norma who no longer bothered to conceal her smile.

"Oh, you'll do nicely," Norma said. She turned to Owen. "Escort her in, and get her a new outfit. I'll spread the word that we have a contender."

Valerie stood and offered a hand to the guy on the ground, but he pushed it aside and stood on his own. Poor guy was already getting a few snickers from the others. He'd lost to a girl, and fairly quickly. It probably didn't happen too often.

"You didn't tell me you could do that," Owen whispered as he ushered Valerie from the room and into a side-hall. "I mean, I just assumed, what with your other talents and all…" His eyes darted down to her chest and Valerie put a finger inches from his face.

One eyebrow raised, "Watch it."

"Hey," he held up his hands, caught, "after what you just

JUDGMENT HAS FALLEN

did to that guy, you better believe I'm going to watch what I say around you." He laughed nervously, looking both ways down the hall rubbing his hand back through his hair. "Shit, I can't imagine what he's thinking right now. I ain't never seen him bested like that before."

"Yeah?" Maybe she'd have to slow it down, if she hoped to keep her cover. Take a few extra hits, next time. "So, I'm guessing this is some sort of fight thing then?"

"Pretty much." He scrunched his nose. "I'd normally say you shoulda went for the red light stuff, better chances of survival and all that."

"Chance of survival?"

"That's right. But after watching what you just did? I'm gonna have to move some bets around tonight," he opened a door for her to step in before him before he stepped over to a dresser and picked up the second package from the left, pulled out what was inside and turned back to Valerie.

She raised an eyebrow, unsure what to think of that, and then even more so when he handed her the new clothes. A full-body leather, skin-tight suit, and—the worst part—heels. Well, not exactly heels, but the kind of shoe that made the back of her foot higher than the front, anyway. She hated that stuff. Give her flats any day of the week.

And now she was supposed to fight in these boots?

"You can't be serious," she said, holding them up.

"Best get changed, and fast." He glanced behind him as a roar sounded from the crowd. "The fights don't happen every night, so when they do, the crowd goes crazy."

She was starting to wonder if she'd made the wrong move here. Wasn't she supposed to be staying out of the spotlight? But, then again, if she wanted to get in close and find out not only what Norma and Clive were up to, but if they had any ties that could point her to the CEOs, she had to get on their good side and earn their trust.

With a shrug, she started pulling off her blouse.

"Whoa," Owen said, blushing and then turning around. "I didn't mean—well, jeesh. I'll give you your privacy, of course."

He quickly exited the room, and she had to laugh.

The laugh faded fast, however, when she tried slipping into the leather. How far was she willing to take this? Standing there, barely able to squeeze into this outfit, she contemplated simply going out there, sniffing out the Forsaken, and then dragging them back to HQ by their hair for questioning.

If only it were so simple. She knew that violence wasn't always the best way to get honest, complete answers. She'd have to earn some trust here.

With a sigh, she breathed in and pulled on the leather. It squeezed her body at first, but after a second seemed to be one with her skin. She checked herself out, even twisting over to see her butt, and smiled. *Damn.* She was starting to understand why some girls wore this stuff.

When it came to the shoes, however, she was not sold in the slightest. These things were clunky, and she found herself wondering if she had ever worn anything other than flats. Even back in Old Paris, on the few times her father had made her play dress up for the eventual day that he might need her in court—which never came—he had always given in to her insisting on shoes that were comfortable. It was practical, after all, if she needed to make a getaway.

Now she was supposed to fight in these things?

Good thing she been training to fight for way too long. She would assume this was just one more challenge to make the training more difficult.

JUDGMENT HAS FALLEN

There was a rap on the door, "Ready?" Owen called out.

"As I'll ever be," she looked one last time in the mirror before stepping over and opening the door.

He stepped back in and bit his lip, looking like he was about to cry.

"Really, that's your reaction?" she asked, unsure how to take it.

"Wow," he said, biting his fist. "You sure you don't want to go red light?"

Her eyes narrowed, "You sure you don't want my knee in your sack?"

His head shook left to right as his fist stayed in his mouth for a moment before he dropped it to talk. "I just—I'm sorry. But DA—AMMNN. They're in for a show out there."

The meaning was polite, the method needed work. "Try saying something more like, 'You look like a strong and independent woman, and that outfit is very flattering,' next time. Deal?"

He laughed. "Isn't that what I said? I could've sworn those were my exact words."

She gave him a look, hands on her hips, feeling way too exposed. The black leather was there, but as far as she was concerned, she might as well have been nude. "Can we get this over with?"

"You prefer a whole room gawking at you instead of one man?" he asked. "Sure, makes sense to me."

She looked down the hall, "I *prefer* to have this all be a distant memory."

He smiled and stood aside, motioning for her to go through down the hall first.

"So you can look at my ass?" She scoffed, and motioned

for him to go. "I don't think so."

With a *you-caught-me* smile, he shrugged and led the way. They took a left and he led them past the room with the flashing lights, which was still full of music and had people dancing, but was about half as crowded as it had been.

"How does this work exactly?" She asked from behind him.

"It's pretty simple, mostly people come to watch the regular fights, but they like to mix it in with some women action here and there. It's sick if you ask me, but who am I to judge. As sick as it all is, I'm still here, ain't I?"

She had to agree with him. It was sick, and so was he.

"So I just have to kick some freako' butts," she said. "I can do that. And this Clive character will be there?"

"Oh yeah," Owen said with a laugh. "He never misses this stuff. Just hope you don't get one of the girls that's using. They can be tough."

"Using what?"

He looked back at her, puzzled. "I keep forgetting you're new. Some of Clive's people, they have a special supply of some new red drug. They keep it on the down low, so I don't know what it really is, though it kind of resembles blood."

Vampire blood, Valerie thought to herself. If Clive's girls used it, that meant Clive had a supply.

She had come to the right place.

"Here we go," Owen said, pulling apart two red curtains. She stepped out into a stairway that led down into a pit and was greeted by a loud cheer from the people on the surrounding bleachers.

Bright spotlights shone on the pit, and blood splattered the ground and walls that protected the spectators.

JUDGMENT HAS FALLEN

This was actually happening. She couldn't believe it. The woman inside said to run, that this was barbaric and dangerous.

The vampire inside was uncaged, *bring it the fuck on.*

In general, the vampire part of her won out, and so she descended the steps, one at a time, shoulders back, chest out, eyes forward.

More cheers broke out as she stepped into the pit, and then a man at the far side, on the top stair but partially hidden in a sort of booth, stood with arms out and silence descended, though some whispered the name, *Clive.*

"We have a volunteer!" he said, and the crowd cheered again, quickly silenced by another wave from him. "It's a dark world we live in, one where our freedoms are challenged at every step. A new leadership has taken hold of the city, but they do not rule over us. This, right here, right now, this is *our* night. Let us enjoy it!"

The cheering rose up and this time he joined by clapping, before yelling, "Let it begin!"

From the area beside him, a woman stood, waved to the cheering fans, and descended the steps. This was a huge woman, as muscular as some of the Weres Valerie was used to. Her black hair was tied up in a bun in a way that showed off her muscular jaw-line, and instead of breasts under that leather suit just like Valerie's, she practically had pecs.

The cheering turned to an anxious hum of awed whispers when the woman stopped five feet from Valerie.

"You're a pretty little thing," the woman said. "I'll regret the maiming, but that won't mean I'll enjoy it any less."

Valerie stood completely still, simply waiting.

The woman was clearly used to more of a reaction than that, because now she snarled and charged, pulling back to punch. A quick glance around, and Valerie had to remind herself to put on the show. Make them believe.

The punch hit her in the shoulder and she spun with it, going to the ground. Not a bad punch, but nothing compared to strikes from Weres and vampires. She scanned the crowd, searching out any sign of more of her kind amongst them, then rolled with the kick to the ribs as if it had knocked her down.

Part of her wanted to laugh at this charade, but then again, it was depressing to know that regular girls were put up against this woman hoping for some quick cash or who knows what, and likely left a mess.

That thought angered Valerie, so when the woman lifted her foot to bring the heel down for a strike, Valerie sprang up, hit the woman with a solid punch in the groin, and then swept out her planted leg while head-butting her.

The crowd went wild as the attacker staggered back, blood gushing from her nose as she toppled over at the pain down south.

"Right in the nads!" someone shouted.

"Bruda's a woman, she ain't got no nads," another yelled back.

"That's debatable," the first retorted, followed by laughter and then more cheers as Bruda stood, ignoring the blood but walking with a limp, and came back for more.

Clive's interest piqued, he was leaning forward now, as were his acolytes who surrounded him on each side. It was time to prove herself.

The wood-plank floor trembled with each step of Bruda's approach. Valerie closed her eyes, silently telling the woman how sorry she was for this, and then turned, opening her eyes to see Bruda's knee flying at her face.

JUDGMENT HAS FALLEN

She dodged around to the left and swung out with her right so that her forearm caught the woman in the collarbone, flipping her up and into the air and slamming her onto the floor. The wind knocked out of her, Bruda gasped and looked at Valerie with wide eyes before the punch came—swift and to the point, knocking her out cold.

Valerie hoped it wasn't enough to cause any lasting damage. But hey, the woman had definitely been out for blood, so if it hurt a bit?

Well, that was perfectly fine with her.

For what seemed an eternity, Valerie crouched there, fist still extended, waiting for a reaction from the crowd. She slowly raised her gaze to the front row, where a line of people sat with their mouths open, eyes wide with shock.

She stood, turned to Clive, and looked around at the spectators behind him before she looked back at Clive, a small smile on her face and asked into the silence, "Who's next?"

He tilted his head, considering her, and then started laughing. The crowd seemed unsure what to do, until he stood and shouted, "Bravo!"

Now the cheers started, filling the little arena. She nodded, not totally enjoying this praise for having hurt a normal citizen of Old Manhattan. Well, maybe *normal* was stretching it. She wasn't sure what to expect next, so stood, hands clenched into fists, until Clive waved her up.

"Bring her," he said to the tall man to his right, then turned and exited through a back door.

Standing there, confused, she hesitated until the man waved for her as Clive had done. Several other men and women stood nearby, all staring at her anxiously, waiting, so she went.

The men and women patted her on the shoulders as she

ascended the stairs, still cheering and clapping. When she reached the top, the tall man simply nodded at her and started walking. There wasn't much else she could do but follow.

In the back room, the crowds cheering was still audible, but more like distant waves than the thunder it had been moments before. Clive stood at the far wall, pouring himself a flask of something red. Blood? Valerie stepped closer and sniffed, and was surprised to catch a whiff of red wine—likely a cabernet.

"Imported from across the seas," Clive said, offering her the glass.

She hesitated, and then took it.

"Bruda has been part of the show here for…" He glanced around at the walls, and only then did Valerie notice the various tapestries hanging there. Different animal symbols on various colors, including one with a golden eagle on red, with fifteen black patches sewn on below it. "Fifteen years now. Each mark represents a victory here, a grand tradition carried down from my time with the Toro Pirates, when I lived in a city once called Toronto."

"North of the old border?" she asked, amazed. "Did… Canada survive?"

"Oh, it's quite pleasant there these days," he said, pouring a glass for himself and nodding to his acolytes to leave the room. He went to the corner and pulled aside a cloth, showing various weapons in a glass case. There were a couple short swords, a claymore like she was used to, and items with metal spikes and more. "A lot of Canada suffered like the rest of the world, but what remained became warmer and, in fact, quite lovely. The people, so used to their free health care and other benefits of old, went a bit crazy once the government collapsed, and what you have now is a hodge-podge of

JUDGMENT HAS FALLEN

different nationalities who've taken up in Toro, if the pirate lord will have them."

"Toro being old Toronto?" she asked, her head working on this new information. Now there was this whole larger pirate issue north of the border, or what used to be a border, but she hadn't even considered how other parts of the world would have changed following the great collapse. Her mind had always been occupied with two places—the parts of Western Europe she'd come to consider her old home, and America, where she'd always dreamed of coming.

Clive nodded and adjusted the tie around his neck. It was dark, almost blood red, and went well with the black dress shirt and suit he wore, even more so with the fierceness in his eyes.

"How… can I help you?" she asked, then took a sip of the wine. *Oh God*, she thought, loving the old taste that brought her back to a younger, happier time in Old France.

Sandra would likely kill for a bottle of this.

"I've never seen fighting like yours," he said. "I'll be honest; I love it here. But part of me has always looked for an excuse to return to Toro, to join back with my pirate brethren and sail the seas, maybe the skies."

She waited for him to continue. He didn't, so she asked, "But something's stopping you?"

He nodded, "And that something is power. Here," he opened a hand and waved around the room, "I have all this. But up there? Up there I'm simply a pirate that hasn't returned yet. You see, my crew was lost some years back, and when I found out I could set up shop like this here, I quickly made it my business to do so. But it's not the same." He looked at her, "Have you ever heard the phrase, "A pirate's life for me?""

She shook her head.

SLOAN AND ANDERLE

He shrugged, indifferent to her ignorance. "Well, it's a phrase for a reason. Was even part of a song once, or so I hear." He downed the rest of his wine and wiped a small droplet of it from his lips, then set the glass aside and smiled. His gray teeth showed he never lacked for wine.

"I'm still not seeing where I fit into this," she said.

"No?" he laughed. "You're my ticket home. Win a couple more fights, show me what you're capable of, and I can make you a hero of the pirate world. They'll love me for returning with you, and together we can form a crew like the world has never seen. It's good luck, you know, having a woman onboard."

"That's news to me." She finished her wine too, feeling the effects of it for a second before her vampire healing dealt with the alcohol. None of what this guy was saying gave her any indication that he was either dealing in vampire blood or somehow connected to the CEOs, but it was quite clear that he was part of the problem with this city. All of this underground crime needed to be stopped, fighting, smuggling, and any sort of pirating included. But she had to be sure, so she decided to dig further. "Does your wanting to leave soon have anything to do with the removal of Commander Strake?"

His expression turned to one of suspicion, but he said, "In all honesty, no. I fail to see how the comings and goings of various political or law enforcement type leaders affects me one way or another."

She made a face, as if he was being obstinate on purpose. "The whole 'being outside of the law' deal?" she told him.

He smiled and nodded. "I'm glad you're smart too, though right now you might just want to focus on the being a badass part."

She took a moment to look around, assessing her options.

JUDGMENT HAS FALLEN

Standing up straighter, she turned back to Clive, "I've always been interested in adventure. I'm thinking perhaps the pirate life sounds like just the thing."

He waved his hand, a glint in his eye. "Wonderful! Rest up for now while we arrange for your next fight tomorrow. Cheryl will show you to your room."

Valerie glanced over her shoulder to where a young woman in a similar leather outfit stood. Did all of these warrior girls wear the same clothes? She supposed this could be why they called it the black side—black for the leather they wore. Although, black for death could work too, if most of these fights ended that way.

"And us," Valerie asked Clive, seductively, "when do we get more time to talk?"

He smiled at her and laughed. "Oh, honey, you'd be so lucky. But our relationship is purely a professional one. Prove yourself, help me, and I help you. Simple as that."

She wasn't entirely sure what he meant, until Cheryl had taken her by the arm and was leading her from the room. They passed the tall man from earlier, who was giving her a nasty glare.

She looked at the man and then to the woman guiding her. "They're a thing, aren't they?" she whispered to Cheryl.

Cheryl gave her a *shut up* glance, but returned a slight nod of the head. Hmm, so getting close to this Clive guy was going to really be about kicking ass.

Luckily for Valerie, kicking ass was quickly becoming one of her best abilities.

CHAPTER FIFTEEN

Enforcer HQ

Cammie walked along the halls of Enforcer HQ, the limp nearly gone thanks to her healing powers. She damn well wanted to get back to that place in the sewers with all those traps, to discover what they were hiding, but not anytime soon, and not until Valerie returned.

In the meantime, she was content to follow the plan. Get the forces together, and hit the town. The blood trade had to come to a stop. Anderson and his Enforcers had to be found and captured, or better yet tossed off into the water and told to swim over off the Island or be killed.

Ella, most of all, had to be stopped.

And that was why she kept glancing at Wallace, walking three paces behind Colonel Donnoly, and not envying him in the slightest for his predicament. Behind him walked several other cops, including Peterson, with a group of her closest and toughest Weres behind them.

JUDGMENT HAS FALLEN

Royland and his crew were already out there on the streets. If recent nights' reports carried through to tonight, they were likely doing their fair share of putting down riots and stopping what appeared to be one-off violent attacks, although many at HQ suspected these were being carefully orchestrated.

Cammie turned into the lobby, where more of the Weres and cops waited, and here she paused to turn to Donnoly.

"I need your people at the square," she said. "This gets ugly or people get spooked at the fact that we're out in force, you might need to do some crowd control."

Donnoly glanced over his shoulder at Wallace and waited for a nod from him before saying, "It's a role we're accustomed to. I've also set up twenty pods on patrol to get a bird's eye view of the city, and have some of my best here defending the building, should it come to that."

She nodded and smiled, looking over the group gathered there, cheered by the fact that Donnoly still relied on Wallace for all decisions. Yes, Donnoly held the power, but only because of Wallace. The senior cop knew that Wallace held the good grace of the vampires and Weres, a fact that he was smart enough not to ignore.

"Esmerelda and Presley, you're with me," Cammie said, seeing the Golden City Weres standing near the door. She knew they'd been training in the week since they had arrived, and were itching to get out on the streets. "Felix, can I count on you to gather some muscle and help hold HQ in case of attack?"

The large Were, also a former Golden City resident, nodded and said, "They come knocking, I'll be glocking." He patted the two glocks at his side, earning a quick laugh from Cammie.

"Super lame, Felix," she said. "But I appreciate the attitude."

He laughed and said, "You prefer I salute and say 'SIR, YES SIR!'"

SLOAN AND ANDERLE

"No, I'll take the lame jokes. Save the formalities for the colonel here." She nodded to Donnoly with a smile, then looked at the rest of them. "Duran, you have your team?"

"Sir, YES SIR!" Duran smirked, but quickly ducked as Cammie pretended to throw a knife at him. He straightened, smiling nervously, and said, "I mean, you got it boss."

She looked to Donnoly and said, "You're up."

Donnoly stepped forward so that he was in the center of the room. "Okay, here's the deal. This city has seen its fair share of violence. Did it see more peace in the time of a violent dictator? Arguably, but not so for the people he put down, hunted, and tortured. And yes, I include vampires and Weres in the term people, because we must. We are all people, and we are all citizens."

Mumblings of agreement went up from among those gathered, and a couple cops shouted, "That's right," or "Damn straight!"

He looked around, "Well, there's a shit storm and it's raging out there," Donnoly continued. "This is our city, and we mean to take it back. We will find Anderson, we'll flush him and his little rats out of hiding, along with anyone and everyone who has betrayed us or besmirched this great city. But we don't need *heroes* out there. We are a team, got it? You come across Weres that are still on the other side, or same with vampires, make a call. Find Royland or Cammie, and get the right people in there for the job. Do I make myself clear?"

"SIR, YES SIR!" everyone yelled together.

He nodded his approval.

"Then get out there and take back our city, dismissed," he finished, standing straight himself.

Cammie gave him a nod to show she approved, and then nodded for her crew to follow close. Esmerelda and Presley stuck close as they exited the building and descended the stairs, the others doing likewise as more police pods dispersed overhead. But at the bottom of the steps, Cammie paused at the sight of a broad-chested man, walking toward them like he was a boulder rolling along to knock them down.

"You Cammie?" he asked.

She stood her ground and asked, "What of it?"

"Valerie said I should join up," he said. "Something about helping to fight the real bad guys. Well, I'm game." He glanced at those with her, "Name's Dreg."

"We're kind of in the middle of something," she said, but sniffed, and paused. "Were, huh?"

He nodded. "Bear."

"Damn." She scrunched her nose, hating the idea of turning down a Werebear, especially if Valerie wanted her to take him in. "How do we know she really sent you?"

"Would I know to say she did if she hadn't?"

"That's not a bad point," Duran said, pausing nearby. "You want me to take him in my group? I could use the muscle."

Cammie assessed the guy, and then asked him, "You comfortable on the streets? Ready to get to work right away?"

"Do I look like I came here for a spa treatment and a nap?" he scoffed. "Point me in the direction of someone you want answers from or want dead, I'm your Were."

The male voice became teasing and pleading, "Can I *PLEASE* have him? Pretty Please?" Duran asked, "With a steak on top, and beer, and more steak?"

Cammie rolled her eyes and shook her head, "Fine," she told him and hiked a finger over her shoulder, "Newbie, you're with Duran. Stick close, and make sure none of my people are harmed. You do that for now, and I'll consider you one of us when we get back. Understood?"

SLOAN AND ANDERLE

"You're the boss," he said, and accepted Duran's thanks as he welcomed him to the team.

With a nod from Cammie, they spread out into the city.

❖ ❖ ❖

Old Manhattan Streets

Royland perched on the ledge of a second story balcony, watching as two of his vampires approached a man on the street from different angles. The man had been one they had been trailing for a few hours now, waiting to catch him in the act.

It looked like they just had, as he was pocketing money he'd just received from a woman who one of Royland's other vampires had split off to pursue.

The man and woman weren't the real concern here though. This was all about finding the central point, the bar where the blood was being dealt or funneled through.

How Royland had ended up here, leading a group of vampires for the good of the city, was still a bit beyond him. He'd been a Forsaken, after all, and a leader of his clan at that. When they'd been wiped out and he was caught by the hunters, then bled for this blood trade.

He had known he was done for.

But redemption came in the form of a vampire from across the ocean. A vampire named Valerie, who he would forever owe his life to.

He stiffened, ready to move as the first of his vampires confronted the man. It looked like they were about to make a deal, but then the man ran. Here came the second vampire fast, blocking the man's path.

Royland leaped down and stood waiting, as the man

JUDGMENT HAS FALLEN

turned and darted his way.

"Step aside, clown," the man said, charging right for him.

With a shake of his head Royland spun with the man, lifting him into the air, and then slamming against a nearby wall.

"Your supplier, if you want to live," Royland hissed. "Where?"

"You ain't cops," the man spat back. "So I ain't talking."

"The fact that we're not cops means you have all the more reason to talk." Royland wanted so badly to reveal his fangs or glowing eyes, but that went against their purpose out here. Instead he used his enhanced strength to lift the man into the air with one hand, and then pull a long blade and tap the man's gut with it. "Start talking, or I spell out a message with your entrails for the next dealer to find."

The other two vampires stepped up behind Royland, and the man whimpered. Even more so when another vampire appeared, dragging the woman over by her jacket.

"The blood?" Royland called out, not even looking over his shoulder.

"Three vials of it," the vampire who'd brought the woman replied.

"Please," she said. "It's for my sick mother she—"

Royland growled and tossed the man so that he landed roughly next to the woman, earning a shriek from her.

"Justifying the hunting and torturing of some to help others who are sick?" Royland asked. "Sorry, but that will never work for me."

The man staggered backwards, pushing with his legs, but one of the vampires was at his side in an instant, pinning him down with his boot.

"Last chance," Royland said.

The man cast a nervous glance down the alley, to a set of

wide, metal doors that resembled more of a loading dock than anything else.

"Right there?" Royland stepped forward, picked him up, and shoved him toward the doors. "Great, make an introduction."

His voice went up an octave, "They'll kill me, man."

"Them or us. At least this way, we'll be there to distract them, give you a running head start."

With only a moment's hesitation, the man started walking towards the metal doors. He glanced over his shoulder and told him, "You can let her go. She's just a customer."

"I imagine she'll have information on other suppliers than just you, so," Royland motioned him onward with an annoyed glare, "hurry this up."

An awkward glance passed between the dealer and his client, and Royland was pretty sure there was something more there than they had let on. It probably had something to do with why the dealer cooperated. He led them to the doors and then, after a moment to pull himself together, pulled one open.

And went flying back through the air as an arc rod connected, blue arcs of electricity flashing in the night.

Royland's eyes went wide. That was certainly unexpected. Amid screams from the woman, three men in old Enforcer Uniforms stepped out, arc rods hot with electricity.

"Looks like you boys stumbled along the wrong alley today," one of them said, and then struck for Royland.

"You all need to get back to your cages," Royland said as he jumped back and out of the way of the arc rod.

"We figured it's easier to kill you all from out here," the man said, and then swung again. This time Royland caught the arc rod at the base, though it still sent a shock of electricity up his arm. He brought his other arm up and snatched the man's arc rod out of his hands, then blasted him across the temple with it.

He looked up to continue the fight, when several more appeared, rifles and arc rods in hand, and in their midst in the doorway—the former Colonel Anderson.

"An old reunion," a female voice said, and both groups looked up to see Cammie on the rooftop of a two-story building next to them.

"This is that Enforcer jackass?" Another Were woman had appeared next to Cammie, and Royland thought he recognized her from the Golden City Weres who had recently joined them. "He doesn't look so tough."

"Come on down and find out," Anderson said.

"We'd love that, wouldn't we, girls?" Cammie said, and a couple more Weres appeared from the shadows in the alley, others on the rooftops. "Don't mind if we join you, do you, Royland?"

Royland put the arc-rod under his arm for a second, and pulled on each sleeve before grabbing the arc rod once more and responded. "Good to see you, Cammie. I was just about to take out the trash."

"Oh, then by all means." She jumped off the roof, her boots hitting the concrete making a loud thump. She walked up to Royland and patted him on the shoulder, never taking her eyes off of Anderson. "Let's kill some pieces of shit while we're at it."

He laughed at Anderson's frown, and said, "She's really horrible at these metaphor things. It's kind of her thing."

"It's true," Cammie said. "You know what's more my thing? Tearing the heads off of assholes like you, Anderson."

"Again," Royland said, holding a finger thoughtfully in the air, "you see how that's a weird image, right? I mean, technically assholes don't have heads. Just, you know, pointing that out."

SLOAN AND ANDERLE

"Royland, can we just kill him already?"

"Anything to make you happy," Royland said, and smiled at Anderson. "Ready to die?"

"What's wrong with you all?" Anderson said, completely flabbergasted. He looked around at the force arrayed against him, and then shook his head. "Another day, perhaps." Then he stepped back, pressed a button, and the metal doors slammed shut. Three former Enforcers stood there, completely surrounded by Weres and vampires, and one pissed his pants.

"You three, drop your weapons and you live," Cammie said. "Presley, get us in there."

As Presley went to pull at the door, the others circled the three men who were now lowering their weapons.

"What, we're supposed to go lock them up again?" Royland asked. "Easier to just…" He saw the look in Cammie's eyes and said, "Okay, okay, we got them."

The doors slid open, but when they ran inside it was empty. Just a wide, open space that could have been set up like a bar, but wasn't now.

"Where the hell'd he go?" Cammie asked.

Royland sent his vampires to the far ends to look for escape routes, and then he looked up and saw the flashing light before he realized what it was.

"Eat shit," one of the Enforcers said from outside, and ran.

"Get out!" Royland shouted, and he pushed himself to the limits, diving for Cammie so that he could throw her into a corner and shield her body with his own. The explosion came a split-second later.

The ringing in his ears was strong, but nothing compared to the pain as the flesh on his back boiled and moved with the flames. Someone was on him, covering him with a cloth and shouting, but all he could do was curl into a ball and do his

JUDGMENT HAS FALLEN

best not to scream.

He was distantly aware of Cammie there, and through the ringing in his ears he heard her thanking him, holding his face and saying, "Oh, God!" as she put her forehead against his. "Hang in there, Royland!"

❖ ❖ ❖

Cammie stood, letting the others take control of Royland now that the flames were out.

"Go, find the nearest police pod you can to get him back to HQ," she demanded, but when she noticed Esmerelda looking past her with a horrified expression, she spun and saw charred flesh among the scorch marks from the explosion. "Who was it?"

"One of the vampires," Presley said, coming up beside her with a hand on her shoulder. "The rest of us were at the doorway, and Royland's warning gave us just enough time to escape. Barely."

Cammie looked down now and saw burn marks on Esmerelda's pants, but her legs beneath were unharmed. Others had burn marks, a couple that were outside were completely unharmed, and still held the Enforcers in their grasps.

Breaths coming out heavy now, Cammie turned to the Enforcers and marched over. At the first, she punched him until there wasn't much left of the man. She stood and turned to the second, blood dripping from her knuckles, and said, "These bastards with their bombs, with their sneak attacks... this shit's about to end!"

She stepped forward and was about to attack again, when the police pod interrupted her anger so she turned around and watched Peterson jumped out. "Where is he?"

SLOAN AND ANDERLE

Cammie gave a furious look back at the Enforcer, and told him, her eyes flashing in the night, "You're lucky, for now. But if you don't talk immediately, you're for *dinner*."

The Enforcer's eyes went wide and he looked about to faint, but Cammie turned from him and led Peterson to Royland's side.

As they knelt to help him up, the vampire who'd been taking care of him backed off now to lean against a wall and catch his breath, Cammie turned to Peterson and told him, in no uncertain terms, "If your sister's working with Anderson and had anything to do with this, she's as good as dead."

Peterson ground his teeth, "If she did, I'll see to it myfuckingself," he said. Careful with Royland's burns, they managed to get him into the pod.

In the distance, another explosion sounded, in the direction of Capital Square. They shared a look of worry, and then Cammie said, "Get him cared for. A couple of vials of blood, at the very least."

"On it," Peterson said, and then he looked over Cammie. "You didn't get hurt at all?"

She rubbed her ear, which was still ringing slightly, but said, "No, and I owe Royland for that. More than I care to know."

Peterson nodded, and hopped in the pod. A moment later, they were gone, and Cammie was motioning everyone to follow her to Capital Square.

❖ ❖ ❖

Capital Square

Jackson had been just two blocks away from the square when he heard the explosion go off. He'd just been training Lorain on how to operate a new type of pistol he'd gotten ahold of. He looked over at her and saw her eyes were wild with fear yet still she looked ready for combat, duty bound to go stop what was happening, he nodded and said, "Come on."

They ran toward the square together, darting past people going in the opposite direction, coughing up smoke. Some were injured, limping, others just scared.

"What's happening to this city?" Lorain said.

"Growing pains," he replied. "But I'd say we've about reached our full height."

She looked at him with a frown and then said, "Tell that to the survivors, since you can't say it to the dead."

"I—I didn't mean it like that," he said, remembering her own family. "Just, sometimes violence happens for the sake of progress."

"And in our case, it needs to fucking stop," she replied, looking at all of the people hurt as they ran by.

"Language," he said, scolding as they turned the corner and out into the square. The smoke was still clearing, and the crowd of people was in all sorts of disarray. Some on the ground, holding their heads or other injured body parts, others trying to help, still others in the process of fleeing, but limping due to injuries.

"Somehow, my use of swear words seems pretty small on the scale of what's important or not," Lorain told him. "Given all this."

He had to agree, but just shrugged.

"This is about your girlfriend," Lorain said. "And she's not even here to defend herself, or us."

"Wrong," Jackson said. "This is about idiots doing idiotic things, and they need to be stopped."

She checked her pistol to see that a round was loaded, just

SLOAN AND ANDERLE

like he'd taught her, and said, "Point me in the right direction, I'll be glad to take them out."

They ran forward, searching for any area they could help, when Jackson froze, eyes on the edge of the square. Ella was standing there, looking over it all, eyes wide. How could she do this and then just stand there, watching?

"ELLA!" he shouted, and ran for her as he lifted his pistol. She snapped out of it, saw him coming, and ran.

"Don't make me shoot you!" he demanded. "Do *not* make me!"

He skidded around the corner and had her, frozen like a deer in the headlights. She had a gun, but reached out and placed it on the ground, before kicking it over.

"I swear, I wasn't involved," she said.

And then Lorain shot her.

CHAPTER SIXTEEN

Northern Bazaar

Valerie paced her room—a small trailer in the back of the large area built for the fighting arena on one side, the place for partying and the red light business on the other.

Part of her felt that this was the right track, that anything as underground as this was going to unveil something, but at the same time her mind would bring up the question of how Sandra and the others were doing.

There couldn't have been any attacks on the city, or word would have spread.

At the first sign of a problem, Valerie planned to split, grab her sword and jacket where she'd stashed them, and rush back to help her friends.

In the meantime, she hoped they could hold down the city. This was, after all, part of a larger test for them. She'd taken out Strake, but knew her role was to bring justice to those in need, to restore honor to her kind. It wasn't to run cities. But at the same time, taking out one leader only to let an equally corrupt one take the reins was as good as doing nothing.

These people though, she trusted. Wallace, Cammie, Royland, and the rest. Jackson…

She sat on the bed and bit into an apple from the food Clive had brought in for her. Staring at the blank, white walls of the trailer, she couldn't help yearning for Jackson.

First of all, she'd kill for one of those damn hotdogs right now, and part of it was just that he loved them so much. Maybe she wouldn't kill, but she'd certainly be willing to hurt someone a little for one. Second, she wanted what Sandra and Diego had, and the look in Jackson's eyes told her he wanted it too.

Only, fate wasn't so kind to the two of them.

If they were going to bring peace to this city, his people had to believe that they weren't together. In general, the people of Old Manhattan needed to believe that peace and order were achievable, which meant she had to root out filth like those that lived here and fed off of others. Whether what was happening here involved pain, pirating, or the sex trade with those who didn't want to be a part, it all needed to cease.

But first, she needed answers. She needed to see how it fit in with the bigger picture—the CEOs. Or if it did at all. The worst part about the situation was that if it didn't tie back to them somehow it would just mean to her that so many people were corrupt by nature, and she just couldn't believe that.

She was a vampire. She knew corruption. Yet, she'd refused to let the darkness in.

Standing again, she began to pace the length of the trailer, anxious to get this moving. There were two guards outside.

JUDGMENT HAS FALLEN

Clearly this trust and collaboration Clive talked about had to be earned, and they weren't there yet. But that didn't mean Valerie couldn't find the thin line areas of their trust and work around them.

There had to be a way out of here, to see what more she could learn about this place.

Trailers usually had ways of accessing water, right? She entered the bathroom, a tiny square section of the trailer, and was glad to see they actually had a shower in here too. That could be useful for later, in case she had to make someone bleed and it got on her. But for now, it wasn't much use. The area where the water came in was too small to do much good. She could break the floor, or use her strength to tear the seams around the shower area, but that might make too much noise.

She went back to the small bed and lay back, contemplating, and then noticed the square cracks on the ceiling. No way.

It was easy enough to stand on the bed and reach the small patch of ceiling, and just as easy to push and open the area. It must have been for ventilation or some add-on feature that this trailer didn't have any more, but right now it was a small, square hole, just big enough to fit through. She grabbed the sides and jumped, pausing before pulling herself up. No one seemed to have heard anything, so up she went.

Now outside with only the large tarp and its lights covering the area, she crouched taking in her surroundings.

Where could she start? She was looking for answers, but didn't quite know the questions. How deep was the crime and corruption here? Were the CEOs still involved? She knew these were the high level issues she needed to address, but had no idea what addressing them would mean.

SLOAN AND ANDERLE

So she focused on her enhanced senses. Her hearing instantly picked up sounds she didn't want to hear, such as the moans that helped explain why several of the trailers were rocking, and the sound of a knife as it either cut meat at a butcher's shop or was plunged into some unlucky soul. That might have been a good starting point, but when she turned her head to try and pick up the direction of the sound, it was gone.

Her eyes saw well in the dimness of this place, but that only let her see a group of people milling about at a rear entrance to the building, drinking some of that orange liquid she'd seen earlier and smoking something. Could be innocent, but was more likely to be drugs.

She wasn't here for a drug bust—hell, half the houses in Old Manhattan could serve as sites for a drug bust.

A scent. Faint, but it was there.

Cocking her head, she sniffed again to make sure. To her left, and there were at least two of them—vampires.

Judging by how far they were from Enforcer HQ, she was willing to bet they were Forsaken. This was a lead for sure, seeing as she hadn't expected to find any of their kind here. They shouldn't even be in the city at all.

Staying low to avoid being noticed by Clive's guards, she crouch-walked to the edge of the trailer. No one below. A quick flip jump, and she was in the clear, running toward the scent of the Forsaken.

"Watch the hell out!" a man yelled at her as she nearly plowed into him, and she had to side-step and twist around two others who saw her running and thought it would be funny to stand in her way. Their whistles as she passed nearly caused her to stop and smack them each into the ground, but she was on a mission.

JUDGMENT HAS FALLEN

The scent grew stronger and she pulled back to a slow walk, focusing on her senses. Out here it was darker, less torches and the lights overhead were more sparse, and past the trailers were actual tents. It was like a little village here. A village of creeps who were into buying pirate goods and paying for sex and violence.

When a man walked by with his arm around a young woman, it was pretty tough for Valerie not to tear out his eyes and feed them to him, but she ignored it.

In good time, it would all be dealt with.

A low grunting sounded and she paused beside a tent that looked big enough for ten people, and tall enough to stand. The scent of vampires was strong here, but she hesitated, not wanting to make a mistake and walk in on people having sex.

After a moment of circling the tent, she was certain that the scent was from in there, so she prepared herself to see something she wouldn't want to see, and tore at the back of the tent with extended claws.

"The fuck?" a voice said, and then a sniff.

She entered to see three Forsaken, now standing in various states of nudity, only one fully hanging out. They were all streaked with blood, and when she looked at the ground, she saw why.

Still moaning, but in obvious pain now, was a man who had been stripped and now had various vampire bite holes across his body, along with scratch marks from claws.

The middle vampire sniffed, and then looked at her with uncertainty. "This one's ours, get your own."

"Excuse me?" she said, debating her first move here, but stalling to hear more.

"You're new here, I take it," the Forsaken said. "Here's how this works. Find someone of your own, turn them if you want, or just fucking eat them, I don't care. But as far as Alex is concerned, it's all business. Either way, this one's claimed."

"Right." Her hand went to the spot on her hip where she'd normally find her sword, only now it wasn't there. Of course. "Problem is, this Alex, he passed on a different message."

"Oh, did *he*?" The Forsaken suddenly knelt for the attack.

"Wait, what?" one of the others asked. "We could use her!"

"This is the one," the first Forsaken said to the other two. "The one we were sent for."

"Oh, mother-shit-sack," one of the others said, and then he let his fangs grow and his eyes began to glow red as he charged.

Judging by the way the other had said "*he*" and then attacked, that had been her mistake. Alex, a female, was somehow responsible for these Forsaken coming here and was, what, putting together some sort of an army?

This wasn't the fighting arena where she had to put on a show, it was several bastard Forsaken vampires. So when the first reached her with the intent of killing her or whatever the hell he had in mind, she had no problem simply jamming her fist into his throat, kicking out his knee, and then twisting his head so that she broke his neck.

The middle one seemed to be the smartest though, because as the nude one attacked, he backed up and went to a bag he had lying on the floor and pulled out a pistol.

Valerie swiped an attack aside and tossed the nude Forsaken into the line of fire but, to the other Forsaken's credit, he cursed and didn't shoot until the nude one had dropped to the floor, covering his head.

At that point, Valerie had time to assess her options and decided the best action was straight on. She ran and used

JUDGMENT HAS FALLEN

the kneeling Forsaken as a springboard to leap into the air and bring down a kick that sent the other Forsaken spinning. She kicked back to connect with the kneeling one's face, then sprang forward and hit the pistol out of the other one's hand.

He rolled before she could attack, pulling two blades from his bag and turning to attack. This one wasn't quite like the others—he was trained. He actually knew what he was doing. Up to now it seemed the fights had been fairly easy against these American bred members of the UnknownWorld.

It was now clear that she was going to have to rethink her misconception of them. In fact, she would take it one step farther—find out how much these Forsaken were being trained, and by whom.

She could take a pretty good guess, though.

A knife glinted as he attacked, nearly slicing her neck open. The second move she was ready for. Instead of trying to block it, she simply dropped to the ground as she spun, taking out the guy's legs, and then rolled for the pistol that he'd dropped.

By the time they'd both recovered, she was aiming in on him and he had no chance.

Or so she thought, because this guy had apparently anticipated her move and kicked out at a corner of the tent, so that the top fell in to obstruct him from view.

"Dammit," she hissed, glancing back to see the nude one in the corner, clearly in fear of her.

Fear. She'd forgotten about that little tool, and just as she saw the knife coming from the corner of her eye, she pushed out with her fear. Now the nude Forsaken fell back to his butt, scooting away on all fours, while the effect on the other one had been to cause him to falter just enough in his attack that she was able to duck under the blade, come up on the other side, and slam the pistol into his face.

She hit his wrists hard, causing him to drop the blades, and then swept out his feet so that she straddled him, gun at his temple.

"Who's been training you?" she asked, careful to keep the other one in her peripheral. "Is it the CEOs?"

The Forsaken glared up at her, jaw clenching as he worked to overcome the fear she'd filled him with.

And then she remembered her other powers, the ability to not quite read minds, but sense emotions. In this case, there was a resounding warmth coming from him, which she took to be a big *YES*.

"This is so much bigger than you could possibly understand," he finally said, voice only slightly shaking. "You think you're the new big thing in town, but lady, I assure you, it's going to end with you screaming for mercy."

She scrunched her nose. "The CEOs don't frighten me."

He laughed. "The CEOs? You ignorant little birdy, don't even know when it's time to fly away home."

"Explain yourself before I make you suffer." She pushed the pistol against his skull. "TALK!"

He smiled. "There's no use in explaining the world to the dead."

Something heavy crashed against the side of her head and she nearly toppled over, but blinked and registered the surprise in his eyes that the blow hadn't done more to her. She looked and saw a baton in his hand, that he must have managed to grab ahold of at some point.

The pistol would be too loud anyway, she thought as she pistol-whipped him again and then grabbed the baton out of his weakened grip. Now she saw it was more than that—it was one of those Enforcer Arc Rods, the kind that could put

JUDGMENT HAS FALLEN

a shit-load of electricity through someone.

So she slid the button up to send the blue lines of electricity circling around the tip and stuck it in the Forsaken's mouth, continuing to jam it down his throat until it wouldn't fit anymore. He spasmed a few times, and then it was over.

"That's for hurting my head," she said, rubbing a hand across the spot where he'd clocked her. Looking into his lifeless eyes, she shook her head and added, "Dick."

She stood, slowly, and turned to face the completely nude one. She just stared at him for a minute, annoyed that she'd been forced to kill the other two, and totally confused as to why this one was naked. "Was it some kind of sexual thing too, or…?"

He let his head shift left, and then right, as if debating how to answer, and then just charged. But, when she went to attack, there was only empty air.

She spun, confused, and saw the tent flap to her right open and still shifting as if it had just been moved. The bastard ran from her!

A quick glance at the man they'd been feeding on showed he was still alive. He looked at her with fear, but she shook her head and said, "You have nothing to fear from me. But get dressed, grab those weapons and run, run as fast as you can. Kill if you must. You can survive this night."

Before he had a chance to respond, she was out, pursuing the nude Forsaken. A few drugged out looking men and women were standing in the darkness looking bewildered—likely at having just seen a naked man run past.

When they saw her in pursuit, they kind of shrugged and figured it was some sex-game, she imagined, not even taking the time to roll her eyes.

Her pursuit took her back toward the main building, but

halfway there, she paused, glancing back toward the trailers. Coming from the building she saw a large procession moving toward the trailer she had been in, and right away she knew it was Clive.

Dammit, he was coming for her already.

Eyes searching the darkness, nose sniffing for signs of Forsaken, she came to a realization. She had to play this out, see how many she could draw out into the open until she could get the answers she needed.

So for now, she moved back into the darkness and made for the trailer. There weren't many distractions, and within half a minute she was at the trailer, lowering herself in through the small hole in the roof, and waiting. She glanced back out the front and saw a guard glance her way, but noticed that Clive was taking his time and had even stopped to speak with someone.

That was good news, considering the Forsaken blood that had splattered on her, she now saw in the light of the trailer.

She went to the bathroom and quickly slipped out of the leather so that she could better scrub the areas that she had dirtied, and then hung the outfit on a rack while she slipped into the shower. There was a bar on the side that showed a very limited water supply, but all she needed was enough to remove the stench of death, so thirty seconds later she was drying off and then doing her best to slip into the leather outfit again.

Of course, it was even harder to slip on this time than it had been at first.

So when the knock came on her trailer door, she was still there, mostly nude, pulling trying to twist and get her arms into the top.

"One second," she said, and then finally got the leather on her arms.

JUDGMENT HAS FALLEN

The door opened as she pulled the top over her breasts, zipped up and turned with a smile.

Clive furrowed his brow and looked her up and down before saying, "You seem awfully chipper."

"I was just… working out."

He nodded, appreciating that. "Ready to show me my judgment is still as sound as I believe it to be?"

Mentally, she wasn't ready at all. There was some nude Forsaken out there likely telling more Forsaken, or maybe a CEO henchmen, about her, and she wanted to be tailing him and listening in.

But since this was the next best way to move the plan forward, she nodded. "Let's give 'em a show."

"Excellent."

He held out his arm for her to take and together they descended the steps of the trailer and made their way back to the arena for her second fight.

As they were walking she sniffed and said, "You smell like sex."

He laughed. "Bluntness, I like that." For a moment they walked in silence, and then he said, "After the great collapse, I'm amazed how many people look down on relationships of the type I enjoy. I often wonder if it was like that before, or was love more accepted for what it was back then?" He looked at her, curious, and then asked, "How about you, you're clearly not judging me the way some would. Would I be wrong to suggest that you might have had thoughts about women in your past?"

Yeah, there had been a moment there, oh yes, the thoughts had been there—that it all would have been forced. That Sandra, as her servant, or slave or whatever the hell she had been, would have felt compelled into it.

SLOAN AND ANDERLE

Valerie hadn't wanted it that way. If it were to happen at all, she wanted it to be pure. But somehow, as the years wore on, it all became like a distant dream. A blur as if it might not have ever happened. She'd never looked at another woman the same, and even those thoughts about Sandra had faded, until Valerie had met Jackson and everything had changed for her.

Now though, confronted with this question and far enough away from Jackson that it seemed they'd never be together again, she found her mind wandering back to that kiss, that time long ago when she could almost believe her and Sandra could be a thing.

"Hmm," Clive finally said, and she realized she'd spaced out. "Judging by that distant, forlorn and yet totally full of yearning look in your eyes, I'm going to go ahead and take that as a yes."

Valerie blushed. This was a side of her she'd never shared with anyone, not even Sandra. All she could think of saying was, "Shut up."

He laughed. "Well, let's put that passion into your next fight, and then maybe we can sit down over another bottle of wine and you can tell me all about it."

"That'd have to be some strong wine," she said, wistfully.

"Oh, I have faith that you'll earn it." He looked her up and down, tip of his tongue at his lips. "Ever had a three-way?"

Her head jerked back, looking over to Clive, "Excuse me?"

With a laugh, he elaborated, "In a fight, a three-way fight. Each of you on your own, but three in the ring. Think you're up for it?"

"You have a weird way of asking, let me just say that. But yeah, anything you throw at me, I can take. Just get that wine ready."

JUDGMENT HAS FALLEN

He nodded with an excited smile, then motioned her to follow as he spun on his heels.

If she played this right and got him to drink enough of that wine, maybe the answers she sought would be coming sooner rather than later.

Perhaps one fight and she could get the answers? God, she hoped this place didn't hold new secrets.

CHAPTER SEVENTEEN

<u>Enforcer HQ</u>

Jackson stumbled up to Enforcer HQ, Ella in his arms, shouting back at Lorain to stop apologizing.

"You didn't know any better," he said.

"What's this?" one of two Weres asked, coming out and glancing over him to the injured woman. "You don't have to let us in, though if you ask around, I'm sure you'll recognize my name—Jackson Mercer. This woman is wanted by the police and others, and has been wounded. If we want any answers from her, I suggest you take a look."

"But she's been shot!" the larger man said, stupidly.

"Exactly my point. You have people here better than any excuse for a medical facility. Now are you going to let us in or what?"

Just then a man came running out, and Jackson had to rub the sweat away from his face to see that it was Wallace.

"What is..." He just stared for a moment, and then

JUDGMENT HAS FALLEN

quickly waved the others aside and took Ella from Jackson. He turned to carry her up the stairs asking over his shoulder. "What happened?"

"The explosion, and then, well," Jackson glanced back at Lorain, but decided the whole truth wasn't necessary for now, "she was shot."

"I can see that," he replied.

They made their way up to the elevator. Ella was mumbling something with her arms wrapped around Wallace, who was caught somewhere between torment and trying to be strong.

Jackson had no idea how he would feel at that moment. He had no good feelings toward Ella, but Wallace once had. Were they in love, or simply playing around? Jackson knew that, if it had been love, nothing could make him change how he felt.

They rushed into the hospital wing where Cammie and two other female Weres were gathered around a hospital bed. Royland lay on his side as a cop applied a salve to his back and Cammie helped him sip on a vial of blood.

"Things could be better," Wallace said, noticing the look on Jackson's face. "Let's just hope that whatever Valerie's up to, it's going to change all this. Otherwise, we might have a prolonged war on our hands."

A Were helped lower Ella onto a bed, and then a vampire took a spot beside her to get working on the wound. The pants were torn, and the burns looked painful.

"You were injured in the explosion," he said, and her eyes flitted open, taking him in.

"Sloppy job then," Lorain said with a nasty glare. "Getting hit in your own blast."

Ella gave a slight nod of her head and whispered, "Not me. Not my people."

"I'm putting her out for this part," the vampire said, and

SLOAN AND ANDERLE

Jackson put an arm around Wallace, thinking that might be comforting.

"What're you doing?" Wallace asked, stepping back. "There was something with this woman, but that's long gone. I don't need your sympathy or comfort." He spun around, taking in the Weres. "And shouldn't you be out there trying to prevent more of these explosions? This guy needs three of you hovering over him like guardian fucking angels?"

Jackson cleared his throat, and Wallace made a grunting noise before stomping out of the room.

Yeah, clearly that man had no more feelings for Ella. Right...

"He's right though," Cammie said, standing. "Royland, heal fast, please. At least so I can stop feeling so damn guilty."

"He saved her ass," the one he thought might be named Esmerelda told him, so Jackson just nodded his understanding.

As Cammie walked past, Jackson waved her down. "Listen, my people. They're on standby. Many of my followers are just regular citizens, but we have a couple dozen warriors ready to take action if needed. They won't fight alongside vampires and, sorry, Weres, but... you tell me where we're needed, I'll do my best."

"Alongside, and against the same enemy, doesn't have to be the same thing," she told him and looked back at Royland for a second before returning her gaze to Jackson. "If we can make a show of force around the bomb site at Capital Square, maybe that'll put some fright into them... whoever they are."

"I'll do my part," he agreed, and then motioned to Lorain to stick close.

❖ ❖ ❖

JUDGMENT HAS FALLEN

When the others were gone, Wallace lingered at the doorway, watching Ella sleep. He wasn't sure what he was doing here.

She had abandoned him and the rest of them, all because of her prejudices and a lost cousin who she'd cared nothing about. But feelings weren't always rational, as Wallace realized, standing there, feeling every urge in his body to walk in take her hand in his, and kiss her forehead.

Who was going to stop him?

Certainly not himself, that was for sure. So, he opened the door and went to her side, and was glad to see her eyes open and a slight smile form.

"Is that a drugged up smile?" he asked.

She smiled wider and said in a whisper, "Probably, but I *am* glad to see you."

"I just wanted to tell you I hope you get better soon."

"That's all?" She closed her eyes for a moment, then looked at him again. "So you weren't over there by the door wishing you could come in and kiss me?"

"I, uh…"

"Do it. Come on, do it already."

He frowned, licked his lips and said, "Do you know how much it hurt that you left?"

"Let me think," she said, and then pushed herself up with one arm, reached out and grabbed him with the other, and pulled him in for a kiss. She let out a pained yelp and then a grunt as she collapsed back to the bed, trying to both breath and stop breathing as her stomach was on fire. She put up her fingers, separated by a few inches. "About that much, maybe?"

Wallace shook his head, "You're crazy."

She nodded. "I wouldn't have left if I wasn't a bit insane. But, I have to stick to my beliefs, and my belief here is that they're too powerful to be ruling over us. Any one of them can break us in two like a plaything, and we think that's okay?" She grunted in pain, trying to move as she spoke, so just lay back. "That's the thing, they're weapons. If one of them has a bad day, we all die. We can't allow that."

"And…" another voice said, and they turned to see Royland was up. "Who blew up Capital Square?"

Ella grunted in response.

"Sorry, Royland," Wallace said. "Didn't realize you were awake."

"He's right," Ella said. "I know it, but it's just… something inside me burns every time I get around vampires and Weres. It's nothing personal, Royland. I know that doesn't help any, and the fact that I can't explain it must make me sound like an idiot, but that's how it is."

Royland laughed.

"That's funny?" she asked, and Wallace had to admit he was confused.

"When I think about Anderson and the others, the ones that got me and I wouldn't be surprised if they were behind the other bombing, well… it burns for me too. Just in a much more real way."

He pointed at his back, still covered in burn marks though not nearly as bad now, and laughed again.

Ella chuckled, and then sighed. "Shit. I know you're not all bad. It's just, there was a reason I became an Enforcer in this city, all those years ago."

Wallace hadn't heard this one, and he leaned forward, taking her hand in his. "What do you mean?"

"I'll just say I've known my fair share of Forsaken. They weren't as quiet about themselves as the rest of you all think vampires should be, and well… Let's just say that my blood must be delicious, because those sick bastards came back for it more than once."

"I'm so sorry," Wallace said, holding her hand to his mouth and then kissing it.

"I would argue that to be different," Royland said. "But no, you're right. There was a time when even I was free to feed, back before, when I didn't fully understand. It was like a fog hung over my head, and sometimes it would clear up and allow me to see, and other times it would become dark and a storm would rage within."

Wallace breathed deep, totally lost as to how to take all this. He'd only roughly suspected all of this dark world stuff before meeting Valerie. He'd heard rumors, but to hear it from these two like this? It made the frightened part of him come out, part of him that wondered if he agreed with Ella.

"But," Royland argued, "those days are in the past. If we can educate the other Forsaken as I have been taught, everything could be different. I am proof of that."

With a nod, Wallace stood up. "Well, on that note. You two, get better soon. Chat a bit, but I need to go help. Like you said, Royland, we need to help them. The best way to do that is to stop the violence."

"Wallace," Ella said when he reached the door. He turned to look back at her, "Thank you."

He stared, wondering at all of the little meanings that could be tied up in those two words, and then nodded as he exited.

It was time to get back out in the street.

CHAPTER EIGHTEEN

Northern Bazaar

Valerie stood waiting, doing her best to avoid the sideways glances from the girl, Cheryl. The crowd was already cheering on the other side of those doors, and Valerie found her excitement level to be way above what she would normally think for something like this.

She was here to set things straight, not show off in front of a bunch of shadow-walking strangers.

So then why was she so excited?

"You were really something out there," Cheryl said, and she breathed out after, as if the words had been extremely difficult to say. "I haven't been able to stop thinking about it."

Valerie gave her a nod, and then said, "Thanks."

"Maybe… if you survive tonight, you could teach me a thing or two?"

"If I survive?" Valerie had to laugh at that. "I'll promise you two things right now, okay? I will survive, and if it all works out, yes, I'll teach you."

The girl beamed and Valerie couldn't help but smile.

"You know what?" Valerie motioned her over. "While we're waiting, here, throw a punch and I'll show you a move or two."

"What now?" She stared, totally amazed that this was happening, and then held up her hands to punch. "Like this?"

"Actually, yeah." Valerie was impressed. "Okay, bring it on."

The girl came at her with a right cross that wasn't half bad, but Valerie moved her head to the side while swatting the punch inward, and at the same time bringing her right fist to stop an inch from the girl's stomach.

"You see?" Valerie asked.

Cheryl nodded and biting her lip, mimicked the move as Valerie threw a punch. Only, she didn't stop with the return of a punch, and her knuckles connected with Valerie's ribs.

"Oh, I'm so sorry!" Cheryl said, covering her mouth. "Are you okay?"

Valerie laughed it off. "Of course. Just, learn to control yourself."

She showed her a couple more moves, wondering if she would be able to take this girl under her wing after taking this place down.

"You were born here?" Valerie asked.

"Chicago, actually. Couldn't stand the corruption and all that there, so I came here. Ironic, I know, considering that I got wrapped up in all this." She gestured around her, then blocked another strike from Valerie.

"Very good," Valerie said, backing up for another fighting stance. "You know, you don't have to stay here. There're ways to make a living without being wrapped up in this."

SLOAN AND ANDERLE

"Says the woman fighting for a few coins?"

"Says the woman who can get you out of here, if you're interested." Valerie debated saying more, but then added. "I've got big plans."

Cheryl looked contemplative for a second, but it receded in favor of an annoyed narrowing of her eyes. The smile returned just as fast as it had come, and she said, "If it were so simple, you bet."

"Isn't it though? Just tell me you're in, and I'll see you out of here safely."

She was saying too damned much, but there was something about this girl that she liked. Regardless, the conversation ended there because that's when the doors opened and the tall man from earlier gestured for her. Cheering filled the room, drowning out any other noise.

Valerie was being ushered forth, only able to manage a quick glance back to mouth "Be careful," and then she was on the stairs, descending down into the pit, faces in the crowd shouting for her to *obliterate them* and worse.

She reached the floor of the arena, and stood tall. She felt exposed, nearly bursting forth from her leather outfit, but she also felt strong and proud.

Clive stepped out and stood just in front of his seat, and held up both hands for silence.

When the room quieted he said, "A three-way fight, to truly test our new hero," he said, and then gestured to one of the doors nearby. Out came the man she had seen earlier, the one who had been following and who Owen had warned her about. Strangely, he was wearing her coat.

He walked like a bulldog about to lock its jaws around her neck, and when he was close enough, he leaned over with a nasty smile and said, "Found my coat." The cheers were too loud for the others to hear them, but they weren't so loud that she couldn't hear this man.

She glanced up at Owen, sitting not far off from Clive, and he shrugged at the turn of events.

"I don't know what you're talking about," Valerie said.

He pulled off the coat and set it aside, then turned back to her. "Didn't happen to find it outside, then?"

She gulped, realizing that, if this was his jacket, and what Owen had said about this man and how he treated women… Oh! The poor woman he'd been with earlier!

"I'm not going to make it easy on you," she said, eyes flashing red so fast that she doubted anyone had noticed.

"Good, that'll make it more fun." He glanced past her and up the stairs, smiling. "Oh goody, two of you."

Valerie spun to see Cheryl walking down the stairs. "Oh no, that's just—"

"Cheryl the Nightingale," Clive announced, and Valerie felt her color drain.

"Wait, what?" Valerie stormed over to her to ask what this was about.

Cheryl just shrugged and said, "As I said, I had to find a way to make it, to survive. This is it."

"But back there..." Valerie wanted to hit herself for being so trusting in a place like this.

"I'd still love it if you took me out of here," Cheryl admitted. "It's just going to be hard, considering our predicament."

"You two girls ready, or need to use the potty together first?" the guy said. Up close and without the coat, she saw how tough this guy really looked. His muscles were jacked up in the way that only someone using some sort of supplement could look.

SLOAN AND ANDERLE

"Shut your hole, Trent," Cheryl said, and then took a fighting stance.

Valerie was still pissed at this seemingly innocent girl being one of the two to fight her, when she sensed Trent charging from behind. The crowd roared, and Valerie spun out of the way, landing a mule-kick on his rear that sent him sprawling.

Next came Cheryl, and it was clear she'd been holding back in the room before. She moved quick, coming at Valerie with a barrage of punches and kicks that seemed to only be possible if she was a vampire or Were, but Valerie sensed neither from her.

Each strike met Valerie's blocks, but when she spun out of the way of a roundhouse kick to the head, still debating whether she should just drop these two and be done with it, she saw Trent catch Cheryl with a punch to the jaw.

Cheryl collapsed to her knees, then barely brought her forearms up in time to block a knee to her face. She grabbed him by the balls with one hand, behind the knee with the other, and took him to the ground as he howled in pain.

So they were attacking each other too, huh? Valerie circled, watching as the man tried to elbow Cheryl on the top of the head but she took it in the shoulder in order to get close enough to land two elbows on his left eye, drawing blood and causing it to swell instantly.

Damn. This girl could be valuable if she was on the right side.

Cheryl rolled off of him and came at Valerie, like a little wolverine clawing and biting, but now Valerie had decided her move here. She backed up with each attack, simply swiping them aside, catching Cheryl off guard when the girl expected the follow-up punch to come that Valerie had shown

JUDGMENT HAS FALLEN

her into the other room.

Trent was back up now too, and he tried to catch Valerie off-guard, but she simply rolled out of the way and the other two collided again in a series of punches, kicks, and elbows that left them both staggering back.

This was kind of fun, actually, Valerie thought with a smile. The crowd was oscillating between cheers when a strike would connect, and laughter when Valerie would dodge out of the way.

"Kill them!" someone shouted, and Valerie glanced back to frown at said person, Past the crowd, the back doors were open and several people came streaming in, looking pissed. The worst part was that one of them was pointing at her and shouting. More followed them, until there were at least twenty. They started pushing their way toward her.

One sniff and she confirmed what she'd suspected—Forsaken. Likely the nude vampire had found clothes and his friends, and now here they were, out for blood.

Her blood.

A strike hit her upside the head and she stumbled slightly, having gotten distracted and not paid attention to the fight at hand. She turned to see Trent's fist inches from her face, so she grabbed it and twisted, snapping the wrist with a sickening CRUNCH!

Trent gasped in pain, and right then she recalled what Owen had told her about this man, and what he did to women. The thrill of the fight was gone, this was about justice. So, as Cheryl moved in for the attack on one side and the Forsaken approached from the other, Valerie made a decision.

It was time to end this.

She kicked Trent in the stomach, doubling him over, and then came down hard on the back of his head with a downward elbow. He fell to the ground, limp and lifeless.

The crowd gasped, and even her attackers paused. A look of fear passed through Cheryl's eyes, and she took a step back.

"Everyone back to your sex and drugs," one of the Forsaken shouted as he leaped over the small barrier and into the arena. "You're not going to want to see this."

Nobody moved.

The Forsaken stood a good two feet taller than Valerie, his hair slicked back and fierce tattoos along his neck. More were joining him now, encircling Valerie. While the crowd didn't run from the place, they certainly scrambled to move farther back and away from the certain bloodshed.

"Here you are then," the tall Forsaken said. "The one they call Valerie, invader of this land."

There was a murmur from the crowd as they all realized who she was, her cover blown. A glance up to Clive showed he wasn't happy with this revelation.

"The CEOs sent you?" she asked.

He just smiled. "What does my answer matter, when you're dead?"

With a flick of his wrist, four Forsaken charged. She took a step back, not worried in the slightest until she saw the flash of silver.

One of the Forsaken had drawn two blades, and then she saw another do the same. Small knifes with serrated edges on one side, the entire blade lined in silver. She would've loved to have her sword here right now to show them what a real knife looked like, but she would have to make do.

She was faster than them, but with four attacking from all angles, and another moving in from the circle, she realized this was possibly the deadliest predicament she'd ever found herself in.

JUDGMENT HAS FALLEN

With a shout of frustration, she pushed fear out into them, and they faltered. But even with hands shaking and eyes full of fright, they came at her. These sons of bitches had been trained, and trained by the best.

Not only was she certain the CEOs were funding them to obtain these weapons, but she had a feeling that Donovan's own had a hand in the training. Why they were here, she would've loved to know.

Regardless, she intended to live long enough to ask questions and ensure she got her answers.

Her plan with Clive was ruined, her hopes of helping Cheryl dashed against the rocks of the girl's own stupidity. With this group of silver-wielding, trained Forsaken, she could stay and try to fight and maybe win… Or she could run like hell and come back for a battle the likes of which this city had never seen.

Mind made up, she charged the tall one, pushing extra hard on the fear and letting her eyes glow red and fangs emerge to get the full effect. Those that could see her screamed and ran, and the Forsaken in her path made attempts to strike, but she was fast enough to block one, disarm the next, and take the third's weapon to use against the tall one.

When she reached him, his eyes were glowing red too and he pulled out a pistol to shoot her. His shots rang out, taking down his own Forsaken as she dodged around them, and then she slashed at him with the blade—not a killing blow, but one designed to force him to step out of the way.

Her path was clear, and she ran. Everything about running like this pulled against her nature, but now she knew her enemy, she knew where to strike. She just needed her friends and her sword to make the killing blow.

CHAPTER NINETEEN

Enforcer HQ

Royland had just attempted to stand. The skin on his back was not pulling like it had been before. There was searing pain, sure, but he didn't mind a little pain. It was lying in bed and missing all the action that he hated.

"Ready to get back out there, are you?" Ella asked, sitting up in her bed and glaring at him. Her leg was wrapped up in bandages soaked in red. Not the best medical care ever, but the best anywhere around here.

He sat up, cringing, and then let out a low groan before turning to look at her. "Why are you here?"

"It's not by choice, I assure you."

"No, I mean… you're so against my kind, why are you sitting there, when you could be trying to find some way of killing me and then fleeing this place?"

She starred for a moment, shrugged and looked away.

JUDGMENT HAS FALLEN

"Having second thoughts?" he asked.

"Me? Never." She adjusted, trying to escape the discomfort. "But I can not want your kind ruling me and walking around unchecked, and still not want to see you dead."

"You're going to have to see a lot of us dead if you want to keep us behind bars, or under house arrest, or… What exactly do you propose?"

She breathed out deep and stared at the ground. "I thought I knew, but honestly… I'm not totally sure anymore."

"I see." He threw his legs over the bed and attempted to push himself up again, glad to feel he could almost move. "Well, just remember that this city will be safe soon, and when that day comes, it will be because of *people* like me."

"You mean vampires."

"I mean people, as I said. Genetically modified? Yes, but people. Valerie has taught me that."

Ella scoffed, but she didn't look totally dismissive, at least.

A shout came from down the hall, and then the door slid open and Cammie entered, shouting at two Weres behind her, "I can walk my damn self!"

"Ma'am, we need to get you checked, there could be—"

"I know, dammit! But quit pampering me like a baby and just get the damn bullet out!"

Royland was up in a minute, eyes drawn to her right side, where she held a balled up shirt someone must have given her. It was drenched with blood. "You were shot?"

She smiled and cocked her head to the side. "How kind of you to notice."

"Come on," he said, ignoring the harshness in her voice. He guided her to the bed next to his, and sat her down. Taking a medical kit from the nearby table, he knelt before her, barely cringing from his own pain as he leaned in to have a look at her wound. She moved the wadded-up shirt and revealed that the skin was actually healing over the wound already.

"We have to get the bullet out," he said, looking at her to see if she'd bite his head off. "I'm going to open up the skin."

Cammie grunted, "Just get it over with already."

"Hang in there." He first took a sterile blade and cut the wound, doing his best to ignore her growl of pain. Next he went to work on the bullet. She cringed with the shock from time to time, and there was a trickle of blood coming down her chin from biting her lip.

"Where were your guards?" he said, trying to distract her.

"Guards?" she hissed out.

"We're not her guards," Esmeralda answered, appearing at the doorway. Presley followed behind her and leaned against the doorway.

"Didn't I tell you to find Duran and report in?" Cammie said with an angry glance over her shoulder. "The city can't afford to have all three of us back here."

"Duran thought it best," Presley said. "Wanted us to get some rest, so we can go in shifts and not all get burned out at once. Said he was following a lead and would get back to us if they needed extra muscle."

"You think you're going anywhere anytime soon?" Royland asked Cammie, and then placed the bullet aside as he looked around for the material to give her a couple of stitches.

Seeing what he was doing, she said, "No need, it'll be healed up soon. Wasn't much but a little bullet to begin with."

He nodded. "Of course. Obviously." Pushing himself up and cringing slightly at his pain, he sat beside her. A glance at Ella showed she'd turned away, not caring to talk with the two or even be there at all.

JUDGMENT HAS FALLEN

Cammie nodded her way with a raised eyebrow.

He shrugged, then whispered, "This city's going to need a major overhaul. It'll get there, I'm confident in that, but I'm strangely confident the path forward will be bumpy."

A weird look went over Cammie's face and she glanced down at her wound. It was already scabbing over, and soon would be as good as new.

"You think we can make this work?" she asked him. "I mean, the vampires and Weres, working together?"

He nodded, slowly, considering. "It's the people we have to worry about. When they find out what we are, will they all react like her," he gestured at Ella, "or can we help them understand?"

"They won't find out."

"I wish I had your faith in that." He stood, went back to the side of his bed, and took another swig of blood from a vial. "In the meantime, all we can do is wait, continue the fight, and hope for the best."

She leaned back, glanced over at Esmerelda and Presley, and smiled. "There's more we can do than wait and hope," she said, then turned to the two ladies. "We're supposed to be recuperating, taking a shift, right? That's what he wanted?"

Presley nodded, not catching on, but Esmerelda smiled.

"We had a custom," Cammie said, standing and walking over to Royland. "Back in the Golden City, when a Were found him or herself lonely, unsure."

He sat the vial down and looked between the ladies. "Yes?"

"Think of this as simply comfort, may it bring you strength to rise above your enemies," she said as she approached him and put one hand on his chest, the other moving across his belt line.

SLOAN AND ANDERLE

He gulped, and was about to say something when he felt more hands on his shoulders, careful to avoid his healing but still injured back. Then Presley walked up to Cammie's side, and the two paused to look at each other, seductively, and then back to him.

"I'm not exactly sure what's happening here," he said. "But something tells me I like it. Only…" He looked back to Ella, who had turned away and, he guessed, was pretending to sleep.

"Come on then," Cammie said, and she took him by the hand and led him out of there, Esmeralda smiling mischievously and Presley biting her lip.

At the door he paused, looking around for his shirt. "Are you sure about this?"

Cammie laughed. "Don't be all prudish about it. Just… take your recuperation as it should be. A time to rest and come back ready for vengeance."

He shook his head, totally confused by the way of Weres, but not about to turn this down for a second. They reached the elevators, and had just pressed the up button when the stairs' door burst open.

It was Valerie. She wore an outfit Royland never would have imagined her in—or at least, if he had it would've been very inappropriate. Leather hugged her body in ways that showed off all the right curves, and her normal well-kept hair was in total disarray, like she'd just stood outside during a tornado.

"Come," she said, "it's time."

He glanced over, wondering if Cammie was going to be annoyed at the way he'd been looking at Valerie just then, but Cammie was too busy checking out the new outfit to care, and didn't seem like the jealous type at any rate.

JUDGMENT HAS FALLEN

"What happened to you?" Cammie said. "And I mean that in the most flattering way possible. Like, seriously, damn. If I had your body and could fit into an outfit like that…."

"Let's focus, shall we?" Valerie was dead serious, though she allowed a half-smile and said, "But yeah, thank you. And Royland, tongue back in mouth please."

He started to protest, but the ladies just laughed. "Honestly, I'm appreciating fine art is all, it wasn't any different than Cammie here looking."

"I'm sure it wasn't," Cammie said with a wink at Valerie.

His mouth open for a second, his brain raced to get caught back up. "Er, maybe I should use a better reference point," he said, and they laughed again.

"Okay," Valerie said, waving them off. "Now that we've got all that tension out of our systems, maybe we can get back to fighting the dickheads?"

"Deal," Cammie said. She checked her wound and it was completely healed now. "Royland might not be completely ready though."

Valerie looked over Royland and frowned. "What do you mean? What happened?"

He rolled his eyes and turned around as Cammie explained about the explosion and everything that had happened since Valerie had left.

"I'm sorry I had to go," Valerie said. "But when we reach our destination, you'll all see why. Royland, if you think you can fight, that's your choice. The burns are healing nicely, but you don't look like you'll want to put a shirt on anytime soon."

"We can all agree on that," Cammie said with a wink.

Valerie looked at her friend, 'Violence and chaos have a weird effect on you, doesn't it?" she said to Cammie, who only looked back at Esmerelda and Presley and shrugged with a fake innocent smile and big eyes.

"I don't know what you mean."

"Right."

Royland, for his part, definitely liked this side of Cammie, though he had to wonder where it came from. One minute she'd been all business, the next she was flirtatious as a dog in heat.

He cocked his head, looking at her, wondering if this was some part of being a Were or something. She just frowned at him and followed Valerie into the elevator.

"Keep up, pretty boy," she said over her shoulder.

He stepped in behind them and asked, "Where are we going?"

Valerie pressed the lobby button and waited for the doors to close before she said, "To war."

Royland pressed his lips together before shrugging, "Oh, good. I always go to war without a shirt."

"I'd give you mine," Cammie said with a smirk, "but I think it'd be a little small."

He smiled to the shorter woman, "Ah, it's the thought that counts."

Valerie looked at the two of them, then to the other two. "Are they always like this lately? Did I miss something?"

Presley shrugged. "Even if she wouldn't admit it, I saw it in her eyes the first time I saw these two together."

"Bullshit," Cammie said. "He's a vampire, I'm just playing around."

"Wait, so to be clear," Royland raised an eyebrow, hands on his hips, "You think of me as lower because I'm not a Were?"

"Now, don't take this wrong, this is subjective, "Cammie

shook her head. "Not really lower, just probably not as good in the sack."

Royland's response was quick and succinct, "*What?*"

Valerie snorted, and the other two just smiled.

"It's nothing personal," Cammie said. "Just, you probably lack a certain animal instinct."

He shook his head in wonder, "Wow, I so hope we live through this so I have a chance to prove your sexist thoughts wrong."

She bit her lip and actually blushed. The doors dinged open and Valerie stepped out, the rest following, but as they did, Cammie leaned over and whispered to Royland with a wink, "Me too."

Royland felt his knees go weak at that, and had to steady himself on the wall. Valerie cast an uncertain glance his way, but then turned to the few cops and vampires on watch in the lobby and said, "Alert everyone. Only the essential few stay behind. I need everyone fully equipped and geared up, ready for the fight of your lives."

They ran off to do her bidding, when Sandra came running in with Karl.

"I'm coming," Sandra said. "There's nothing you can say to—"

Valerie nodded agreement, "Of course you are."

"I… what?" Sandra stopped, trying to assess the new situation.

Valerie smiled. "If I'm bringing the shirtless cripple here," she jerked a thumb to Royland, "of course I'm bringing my best markswoman."

"To be fair," Royland said, "I am going to heal, and will probably be healed before the night's up, based on the amount of blood I drank. Well, war and all, I guess I'll be healed or dead."

SLOAN AND ANDERLE

"Optimism," Valerie said with a chuckle. "And stay at my side, I'll see that you aren't dead. Only," she stopped to frown at him, "how well did you know the other Forsaken clans in the area?"

He shook his head. "Not well at all, aside from the occasional squabble."

"Good, then you'll have no problem killing a bunch of them."

"I don't suppose I would." He looked at her like she was crazy, and then felt the realization dawn on his face. "You're serious? We're going to war with the Forsaken clans?"

"Some of them have been infiltrating the city," she said. "Setting up camp, quite literally. Only thing is, they're armed with silver weapons, and trained quite well."

"The CEOs grip extends far," he replied, already feeling a mixture of nerves and adrenaline preparing him for the fight.

"And I plan on cutting off their hands tonight," Valerie said. "Tomorrow, I hope to get to their heads."

CHAPTER TWENTY

Near the Northern Bazaar

The police pods had been sent out around town to gather up anyone that could be spared aside from a bare minimum needed to keep the city safe, and now they were gathering at the northern wall at the edges of Old Manhattan. Not enough pods to carry all of the police, Weres, and vampires, but still a good number of them. The rest were marching over.

Everyone was geared up, body armor, guns, and arc rods at the ready. If the city saw them like this, they'd likely assume the worst and start a new riot. Luckily, the time of day was also on Valerie's side—it being only three or four in the morning at this point.

But so far this was working out. Cammie and the others had briefed her on the situation in town, and they had all agreed that leaving sentries in strategic locations around the city would do while the main force came here. That, and Jackson's people had no reason to be in this fight, so he had agreed to see to it that his people stood united should there be any problems.

A small army of Forsaken could not be allowed to go unchecked within the borders of Old Manhattan.

The city's defenders were gathered, ready to lay their lives down for her. Sandra was cleaning her sniper rifle, preparing it for major action after already ensuring she was loaded and ready in every other possible way she could think of.

Royland had taken extra blood to help the healing and, though he still couldn't put on a shirt and his rock-hard abs were glistening in the early morning moonlight, distracting Cammie, Valerie was glad he was there.

She even saw Dreg the werebear, nodding at him to let him know she was happy he had joined the winning team.

These and the others were all present, all ready.

Valerie walked over to the edge of the parking lot, behind a tall building where they'd taken to setting up. She sure was happy that she had remembered to change out of those crazy shoes and put her fake Pumas back on, but she had ended up keeping the leather.

It was growing on her.

The lights of the Bazaar were just visible in the distance. There were still people moving about on patrol, others darting here and there, and these were the ones she suspected were making plans to march on her.

They would try to take the city from her, but she had come for them instead.

"Where do you want me?" Sandra asked, walking over to stand beside Valerie.

Valerie pointed out a building not far off, and then said,

JUDGMENT HAS FALLEN

"Come on, I'll get you set up. There's some stuff I want to grab there anyway."

"The sword?" Sandra asked. At Valerie's nod, she added, "Yeah, I kind of wondered about that."

Valerie waved down Duran and told him she'd be right back, but to send over some Weres to defend the building, and pointed it out.

"They'll help defend the lower level of the building if the Forsaken attack up here," she said, walking alone with Sandra over to the building. "But I think they'll be plenty busy enough with us down there."

They made their way over to the building Valerie recognized from her earlier visit here, noting the dark blue sky on the horizon, with a hint of light starting to show.

"We don't have long," Valerie said. "If the fighting gets close to sunrise, I'll have the vampires among us take cover in this building until it's over."

Sandra furrowed her brow, looking over at Valerie with curiosity. "So all this live in the shadows talk? I mean, that basically just happened and we're already out here at war again."

"I've been thinking about that." Valerie paused, turning back to see more pods arriving, staying low to the horizon, which was good to avoid the Forsaken seeing them. "I'm not sure what the answer is yet, but it seems pretty damn clear the CEOs aren't going to simply fade away."

"You want to go after them?"

"To Chicago?" Valerie shook her head. "I have no idea. To leave this place…"

"And Jackson."

"Right. Jackson… we haven't heard much from his people, have we? The ones who split off?"

SLOAN AND ANDERLE

"Not that I know of, but I hear we have Ella," Sandra said. "She was playing a big role in their revolt, and if she's in Enforcer HQ...."

"If she's in...?" Valerie wanted to smack herself. She had seen Ella in the sick bay, even wondered about it briefly, but had she put her sentries in danger by leaving HQ exposed with Ella on the inside?

"I don't think we have to worry about her," Sandra said. "Not really, I mean. I sent Peterson back to stay with her, talk her out of anything horrible. Would she hurt her own brother?"

"We can certainly hope not." Valerie sighed. "All of this, did you have any idea what we'd be getting into when we set off on that blimp?"

Sandra laughed. "Not in the slightest. But... going with you, I knew I'd never regret it."

"Thank you, for that." Valerie reached out and took Sandra's hand, squeezing it gently before letting go.

Sandra looked at her friend a moment, her voice gentle, "You going to be okay?"

"I have the safety of these people to think about," Valerie said. "Me and Jackson? If it's meant to be, it's meant to be. But I can't keep drawing unwanted attention, especially the violent kind, to people who don't deserve it."

She turned to look behind her for a moment, "But for now? Let's just help these bastards find the next life, or the great void or whatever's out there waiting for them."

"Deal," Sandra said, tapping her sniper rifle. "Me and my little friend here are anxious to do our part."

Valerie smiled, and said, "Good, we'll need you, I'm sure. Any Forsaken or Nosferatu come running out, especially toward the city, you take them down.

JUDGMENT HAS FALLEN

Sandra nodded, and then glanced up at the windows of the building. "I'll go find myself a good vantage point. Remember, be safe."

"Don't worry, I've got protection." Valerie pointed to the bottom floor of the building, where she'd stashed her sword. "I just have to go get it first."

Sandra gave her a quick hug, and then scampered off.

The area below the stairs seemed even darker now that Valerie knew what was coming. She entered and then crouched. Moving aside the piece of wall she'd set up earlier, she found her sword and purple jacket, waiting.

"I missed you," she said to the sword, holding the hilt in one hand, balancing the blade on the other. She strapped on her sword belt, put on the jacket, and then took a sip from one of the blood vials. She didn't need it yet, but a little preemptive medicine seemed smart in these circumstances.

All ready to go, she exited the building and found the three Weres Duran had sent. She put them in position, and then returned to the parking lot to assess her troops.

The pods were set up with gunmen ready, and the Weres and vampires stood in rows with weapons at the ready. According to the plan, they would all charge at once, pods from above and in a circle around the Bazaar to ensure no escape, with half the Weres transformed so as to put terror into the hearts of any others that might be thinking of taking up defense alongside the Forsaken.

A smaller group led by Felix, the Were who had saved Diego from the Golden City, was going to raid the Bazaar itself. Since most of what was there was pirated supplies from trading blimps, Valerie didn't have a hard time justifying it. She'd seen the medical supplies and food, and knew what a difference all of that could make to her city.

SLOAN AND ANDERLE

Maybe someday she'd make an attack on the pirates themselves, to see that no trade blimps were ever intercepted again, but this would have to suffice for now.

Taking her place at the front of her troops, she said, "You all stand before me of your own free will. If I am wrong, you are free to go." She waited momentarily, and then added, "That is the big difference between us and them. We do not enslave, blackmail, or harm innocents. The police are led by Colonel Donnoly, the Weres by Cammie, and the vampires by Royland, while Jackson has remained behind to see to the streets.

"But tonight, we act as one. Tonight, we tell those CEO bastards that they can't send enemy troops inside our walls, and that to do so means there will be repercussions."

"Damn straight!" Diego shouted from the crowd.

She smiled at him and nodded. "And tonight, we don't just fight because these bastards are in our back door and mean us harm. We fight because of what they represent. They are the downfall of humanity, the rift between vampires, Weres, and everyone else. Their existence is a smear upon our *honor*, and every heinous act they commit means one more person looking down on members of the UnknownWorld. We cannot let this continue. Not just for vampires or Weres, but for all of us. For the future of this earth and whatever else is out there."

As the crowd cheered, she looked at the stars and wondered what was happening up there at this very instant. It was an entirely different feeling to be wondering when you actually knew *something* was happening.

But right now, her focus was on defeating those bastard Forsaken.

Valerie turned, drew her sword in one hand, accepted a

JUDGMENT HAS FALLEN

pistol from Cammie, and said, "For Honor!"

And they charged, shouting and howling as they did so. Some of the Weres had transformed, including Dreg the bear, and it was a sight to behold. Valerie ran at their head, shouting just as loud as the rest.

Halfway there, a force of Forsaken came out to confront them, as she had suspected they would. They were here for her, after all. Why would they run or hide? And judging by the bit of fighting she'd seen so far, they were the elite. They likely believed they could take her and her army.

How horribly wrong she was about to prove them to be.

The Forsaken charged up the hill, some stopping to fire their rifles, some dropping as Valerie's side fired back. A sniper shot rang out in the night and a Forsaken in Valerie's path fell as its head exploded.

"That one was mine!" Valerie shouted back toward the building where she knew Sandra was taking aim at the next one. She'd better hurry, or Sandra would take down every one of them that stepped close.

Pushing her vamp speed to match that of the Forsaken, who were now darting around the battlefield, she then pushed it to the next level so that she was twice as fast as any of them. Her silver sword gleamed in the moonlight as she cut through Forsaken flesh, removing limbs and heads as she cleared a path.

Ahead, she saw people fleeing the Bazaar from the rear, so she paused long enough to spot Felix moving around the main fighting to intercept the supplies they planned on confiscating.

People were shouting and screaming from within the tents, and she knew it must be chaos down there. And then she saw why—several of the Forsaken were attacking the people from the Bazaar.

SLOAN AND ANDERLE

A sniper shot sounded nearby and she spun, seeing the Forsaken's blade inches from her face. He collapsed, weapon clattering at her feet.

She spun, looking for the tall Forsaken who had led the attack on her in the fighting arena, but he was nowhere to be seen. A tall one like that would be impossible to miss out here, unless he had already fallen. Since she was pretty damn sure he was the one with the connection to the CEOs, she couldn't let him escape. And since he wasn't out here, he must still be in the bazaar.

Cammie came charging past her, kali sticks cracking a Forsaken's skull open, and Valerie grabbed her. Spinning and ready to attack, Cammie had glared at Valerie with yellow eyes and snarled, then realized it was her.

"Careful," Cammie warned.

"I need you with me," Valerie said.

Cammie nodded and then whistled. A moment later, Esmerelda and Presley were at her side. "You just tell us who you wanna kill."

"There're more inside, likely the best."

"Understood."

"You can count on us," Presley said, and Esmerelda gave her a curt bow of the head.

Valerie had to remember that these Weres followed Cammie, not her. So she turned to Cammie and waited.

With a smile, Cammie said, "On me," and led the way.

Fighting continued around them, and two Forsaken leaped into their path, only to find one blown to bits by Royland as he appeared from the left, still shirtless though it looked like his back had practically finished healing. Valerie couldn't help but notice the look Cammie gave him as he turned on the second Forsaken, muscles strained as they locked into mortal battle, and then he broke the Forsaken's arm and snapped his neck. A final stomp exploded its skull and Valerie had to cringe.

Cammie, however, was still watching with wide, intrigued eyes, while her two Weres fought off more attackers on each side.

Valerie slashed across an attacker and turned back to Cammie, "Need a rag for all that drool?"

"What?" Cammie snapped out of it and whacked a Forsaken who had just caught Presley with a slash of its claws across her shoulder. A quick glance showed Presley was fine, so Cammie turned back to Valerie and winked. "Usually nudity doesn't faze me, but something about that guy with his shirt off…"

"Enhanced hearing," Royland shouted from twenty feet off. "Don't forget!" He grabbed the arm from a Forsaken attacking him and broke it over his knee before grabbing the head and twisting it. "Not helping me focus, here!"

"I've got nothing to hide," Cammie said as she worked her way over to him, whacking at more Forsaken and pausing to stash one of the kali sticks in favor of a pistol so she could shoot down a couple more of them coming her way. She reached Royland, took him by the hair and pulled him in for a kiss, then opened her eyes and shot a Forsaken who had sneaked up behind him. When she pulled back, she smiled, "For good luck."

Valerie joined them and said, "Really, is this the best time?"

Royland glanced over at the Bazaar, realizing where they were heading. "I'm coming with you."

"No, your fighters need to see you," Valerie said.

He grunted his displeasure at that, but nodded in

agreement. "Be safe," he said to Cammie, and this time he pulled her in for the kiss. Presley and Esmerelda turned to shoot a couple of Forsaken who had risen, while Cammie's hand caressed Royland's chest and abs.

"*Seriously* not the time!" Valerie shouted, pulling them apart and then pointing back up the hill. "Royland, join your men. You two can go crazy in the sheets when there are sheets to go crazy in. Seriously, what the fuck?"

He blushed like a twelve-year-old boy and wished them luck before returning to the main part of the fight. The bear was up there swatting away Forsaken, but several had managed to climb on his back with knifes, so Royland darted over to help.

"You have that out of your system?" Valerie asked Cammie when he was gone.

Cammie winked and gripped her weapons, but said, "I don't know, you look kinda hot when you get mad."

"Ugh!" Valerie turned and started running for the Bazaar, not even waiting to see if they were following.

"See, like right there!" Cammie called after her, and then was with her, the other two at her side. "Just, if I die right now, I at least had a chance to kiss him, right?"

"Since when do you care about Royland?" Valerie asked, slowing now as they reached the first tent, the one that led into the others. There was no guard now.

"Since the explosion, that started it. Then I got shot, and I started thinking that this could really be it. You know, Sandra has Diego, you have Jackson, and—"

"Well…" Valerie shrugged, then pushed in through the tent flaps and looked around as she said, "Let's just admit that one's complicated."

They were back in a massive tented area, and it was

clearing out fast. Felix and his small band of fighters were in a bit of a scuffle with some of the merchants, but some of the Weres seemed to already have taken over the table with the medical supplies.

Rumors were going to come out from tonight, stories of the UnknownWorld, but that couldn't be helped. If they couldn't keep the people of Old Manhattan alive and otherwise safe, what did it matter if they knew about vampires and Weres?

Valerie realized there was only one place the tall Forsaken could be—the arena. And if she had to bet, she imagined she'd find Clive and Cheryl in there too, if they had taken his side. That, or they'd likely fled.

As they approached the arena, a commotion arose and a dozen women came charging out, chasing down several Forsaken. They carried swords or wore clawed-gloves, and their steel flashed in the dim light. At first, it wasn't clear what was happening, but then Valerie saw the woman, Norma, and she realized these must be Norma's Slicers she'd heard so much about.

They were fighting back! If even the corrupt in this city stood up to the Forsaken and the CEOs, maybe they had a chance after all.

It couldn't be as black and white as she'd thought, but that didn't mean they'd get off without answering for their crimes. She'd leave that part to Wallace and Colonel Donnoly though.

For now, she and the other three charged forward and joined in the fight.

"You?" Norma said, watching Valerie cleave into the vampires. After her initial moment of shock, she nodded back to the arena building and said, "Clive's in there, and he's in trouble. Go, we can handle this."

SLOAN AND ANDERLE

Valerie frowned, but nodded and made her way past the main doors, where just that evening she'd passed in a totally different capacity. She was no longer looking for answers, unsure.

Now she was simply ready to kick ass.

She walked in, standing tall with the three Weres close behind.

In the dance room, the lights were still flashing, the music still playing. Several Forsaken seemed to be on their way out for the attack, but when they saw her, they smiled and retreated back through the door to the fighting pit.

"This feels..." Cammie started, looking for the right words.

"Ominous?" Valerie said.

"I was thinking more like 'fun,' but yeah, maybe a bit of ominous and fun thrown in a bowl and mixed up real good?"

"I think your head's mixed up real good," Valerie said with a chuckle. "Let's just get this over with."

"Agreed," Presley said.

As they walked up the stairs, she expected she'd hear creaking if not for the loud music.

When they stepped into the fighting room, Esmerelda gasped. Valerie just stared, not caught off guard in the least. Men with knives and guns lay dead in the bleachers, many who she had seen with Clive earlier.

Clive was still alive, but he and Cheryl were in the middle of the room, the tall Forsaken standing over them, with Anderson, the former cop, at his side.

"I told you she'd come," Anderson said, his gray eyebrows casting a menacing shadow over his eyes. He smiled at her like they were old friends, and then held out his arms. "Come, Valerie. Join your friends here."

"Friends?" she asked, looking Clive and Cheryl over. She

didn't want to see them dead, but calling them friends was a bit of a stretch.

"Surrender, or they die," the Forsaken said.

"We're already dead anyway," Cheryl said.

Anderson hit her upside the head. "Shut up!"

"Shouldn't have done that," Valerie said. "Were these two my friends? No. Will I be okay with you hitting a girl while she kneels unarmed before you? Hell to the No."

Her eyes glowed red and her fangs had grown without her even realizing it, and she charged forward, sword at the ready. Anderson backed away, but the Forsaken smiled and motioned to one of his minions. Suddenly doors were opening and Nosferatu were charging down for the attack, along with the other Forsaken.

Anderson had a pistol out now, too, and was laughing as he aimed in on her, but he didn't have time to fire. The Nosferatu weren't concerned with who was in their path, only that there were others than their master, and they meant to kill them all.

Shrieking as three of them converged on him, tearing him to pieces, Anderson fell.

"Get out of here!" Valerie said to Cammie as she charged forward, pushing her fear and swinging her sword, and going all out in a mad fight to reach the tall Forsaken.

When she heard the sick crunch of dying Nosferatu, she knew Cammie and the two Weres hadn't gone, and that brought her comfort.

"Remember," Esmerelda said as she took down a Nosferatu, "we follow Cammie's orders, not yours." She spun and took out another. "She didn't say anything about leaving."

Presley leaped past them as she transformed into a wolf, and then Cammie had transformed as well, and Valerie was

SLOAN AND ANDERLE

glad—it would be easier to swing her sword and remove heads if her allies were shorter than neck level.

She took out Nosferatu after Nosferatu, and soon they were piling up around her. A glance to her left showed Cammie and Esmerelda exchanging blows with the tall Forsaken, but soon more Nosferatu had gotten in their way again.

There were so many of these mindless beasts, she wondered if there was ever going to be a way through them.

A loud roar sounded, and a thud on the wall. The fighting paused, then resumed. Again the thud, and then a portion of the wall gave way as the bear charged through, Royland close behind.

"I couldn't let you have all the fun!" Royland yelled, his rallying cry a little drowned out as he and the bear charged into the fight.

Now the Nosferatu were falling left and right, at swipes from the bear, shots from Royland, or the wolf attacks and Valerie's sword. With a final swipe, the path was clear. The tall Forsaken stood before her, sizing her up, and then charged.

Did these idiots never learn?

"I am Valerie. One time vampire princess, Now, I am the Dark Messiah's Justice Enforcer. But most of all, I'm a woman who won't take shit from your useless ass."

So she braced herself, sword at her side, and then spun with a strike. He tried to dodge, but she was quick and skilled—years of training outperformed his, and the sword tore into his chest. He staggered sideways, caught himself, and changed direction, coming at her again.

This time she heaved her sword up and made a vertical line of blood to go with the horizontal. He staggered backward, prepared to attack again, wavered a moment, and then fell.

JUDGMENT HAS FALLEN

"There's got to be more fight in you than that," Valerie spat out, sword still gripped firmly. She became aware of the silence, and when she looked around, the previous dead had been joined by mounds of Nosferatu and Forsaken.

The tall one lay there, desperately trying to hold back the flow of his blood as it came out in waves, and managed to say, "You'll never stop the Black Plague. We're coming for you."

"Wait, the what? Are you serious with that name?" Valerie asked, sliding her sword in her sword belt.

"Yeah," Cammie agreed. "It's gotta change. That's lame."

The Forsaken glared at them, then lunged—instead of meeting him half way, Valerie stepped back, kicked out his legs, and grabbed him by the back of his head. With one swift motion, she slammed his head into the floorboards so that they cracked, and then again, sending splinters shooting out around them. One final time, she lifted his head and *slammed* it so hard that it went right through the floorboards and smashed in the process.

Just for good measure, she grabbed one of the splintered pieces of wood, a long, pointed one, smiled at Cammie, and then turned him over and jammed the piece of wood into his left breast.

"A stake in the heart?" Cammie asked, wiping a little spot of blood that had hit her face. "Really?"

"What, you didn't think it was cute?" Valerie laughed and then stood and stomped on the piece of wood, so there'd be no question it penetrated his heart. She looked down, annoyed. "Too bad, the stories say we explode when that happens."

Cammie smirked. "Exploding vampires? No thank you, we've had enough explosions in this city lately."

Valerie had to agree and, as they exited, she drank her

last vial of blood as she looked around, putting the stopper back in and then said, "The city is yours, Cammie. Yours, Jackson's, and Royland's... if you two can keep your hands off of each other long enough to delegate, that is."

Cammie laughed, glancing over at Royland, who smiled back, wiping blood from his perfect chest. "We'll do our best."

Valerie took a moment to survey the damage, "That's all I can ask."

She turned at the movement of something in the corner, and saw that both Clive and Cheryl had survived. A part of her wanted to see them both dead, but she blamed that on her blood lust. Fighting and killing caused people to think in weird ways.

Cammie exchanged an uncertain look with Valerie, but then Valerie nodded.

"Bring them with us," Cammie said to her Weres. "We'll see if their knowledge of the streets comes in handy."

They exited the bazaar and found a battlefield strewn with Forsaken. Several injured Weres and vampires were being helped up by the others, but they would recover. Their strategy of keeping the majority of the cops as marksmen had paid off with minimal casualties.

"You're staying in the shadows then?" Cammie asked.

"I'll check in on you all, come and go. But until we're sure the CEOs are out of the picture and can't pull any more strings here, I can't have Enforcer HQ acting as the lighting rod. If I'm on the move, they won't know where to expect my next strike."

Cammie nodded and turned to smile at Esmerelda and Presley. "You two did good. Now let's get this mess cleaned up. This city's our home, let's make it a great one."

"It's done?" Diego asked, his clothes bloody.

JUDGMENT HAS FALLEN

She looked at him, debating how to answer that question, then noticed Sandra walking over, strong and intense.

"We've dealt a blow to the blood trade, I imagine," she said. "But it's more than that. This was a boulder in the path of whatever plan the CEOs have for us. We've been victorious in that, but they're still out there." She turned, staring out past the city walls.

"Judgment has fallen. They must be dealt with."

EPILOGUE
CHAPTER TWENTY-ONE

Sandra's Café

It was the first café in Old Manhattan, and it was Sandra's. Everything was set up right for the big opening, except Valerie was late. Jackson sat in the corner with a few of his people, while Royland sipped on a glass of the newest import of wine while chatting with Esmerelda and Presley.

Sandra prepared a plate of cheeses, and couldn't resist taking a bite. The way it crumbled in her mouth made her want to just sit back with a glass of wine, stare out at the countryside, and maybe take a nap.

But right now she had a restaurant opening to see to.

Finally, Valerie and Cammie appeared in the doorway. Sandra set down her cheese platter and glared at Valerie.

"Told you," Valerie said to Cammie, hitting her arm playfully.

"Hey, I'm not mad you're late, really," Sandra said but Diego nodded with wide eyes, and she caught him. "I'm not.

JUDGMENT HAS FALLEN

Ugh, whatever. All I ask is for a little order!" Sandra ushered her toward the back room. "I have some chef outfits, you two can get washed up back there and changed, and then you get your asses back out here to help me open this damn restaurant."

Valerie and Cammie turned to her, confused, and Cammie said, "If there's another attack, we need to be out there defending the city against it."

"Screw that," Sandra said. "Delegate. Let them deal with it while you two help a friend."

Cammie chuckled. "Deal."

"I'm proud of you," Valerie said, stepping in for a hug.

"Nu-uh," Sandra said with both hands up to ward her off. "Get to work. Hugging later."

Valerie laughed and nodded, then headed back to get ready for the big day. It was nice, knowing that Sandra was living her dream of seeing some of their world brought over here. Sure, they had to worry about pirates on the trade lanes and the CEOs were still out there, waiting to be dealt with or planning their next big hit.

But for now, Valerie was just going to enjoy some well-earned time with her friends.

AUTHOR'S NOTES - JUSTIN SLOAN

Written: February 13, 2017

Here it is - the TEST! Some people read book one to see what it is, some read book two to give me a second chance, and of course there were the fans who loved them.

Thank you! I say thank you to you, specifically, because I have to assume that if you've made it through book three, then you must be enjoying these books, right?

So if book three comes out and there are no sales... then I go and cry in the shower. However, based on some of the emails I've received and reviews I've read, I am confident that a good number of readers have faith in me.

You know what? That means the world.

This whole writing thing is a blast, but it can be quite nerve-racking. Are they going to like it? Are they going to leave a bunch of one-star reviews saying they not only hate the book, but hope I die a slow, painful death? (I've seen those reviews, though not for my books, I'm happy to say... Please don't!)

What's not to like in these books though, right? I'm there with you, but some reasons I might be concerned include the fact that (a) I'm not Michael, and (b) that I'm not simply trying to copy Michael's voice. Yes, he writes these with me, but you know what I mean.

To address those:

A) I'm not Michael. There's just not getting around

this. As much as I might try, I can't look as good as that guy! Also, we have different tastes. I'm obsessed with Game of Thrones (*Yes he is - Michael*) and Harry Potter. I've watched The Princess Bride so many times that I'm surprised every story I write isn't just an exact copy of that movie. Braveheart too... Back to the Future too.

Haha. I bet if you got his list, it would look pretty different.

B) I have my own voice and style. We're not trying to get a ghostwriting gig here, where I pretend I'm writing as Michael and everything is the same as his other books. Because of this, some readers move on and leave reviews of two stars that say "This isn't Michael," and not much else. I have to laugh at that - Nope, I'm not Michael, and I do have my own tastes and writing style.

Both of those said, he is involved in the books. He helps come up with the concept, provide input throughout, and then does some writing and editing at the end. So if you like Michael and hate me, there still MIGHT be enough here to keep you somewhat engaged.

Let's look at my other writing and see why it might be different.

I tend to write either straight up Disney or Harry Potter style stories (Teddy Bears in Monsterland and Allie Strom and the Ring of Solomon, respectively), or massive epic fantasies where there are gods and mythology and a dragon shifter (my Falls of Redemption trilogy, which starts with Land of Gods).

Do those sound similar to the Kurtherian Gambit stuff? Haha - no way! Though with all the directions Michael is taking the series, who knows, right?

So I'll have some readers check out my kids' stuff and then move onto my fantasy or urban fantasy, and be like "Whoa, these are kind of dark!"

Yes, dark things happen, there are coming of age themes, and sometimes lots of grief before the heroes come streaming out of the darkness with light blasting from their fingertips, just in time to defeat the bad guy and save the world.

I feel that's a bit different from what we have with Valerie - a woman who is going to kick butt, and more butt, and more butt.

Right?

So yes, getting back to the point, I am VERY curious to see how readers accept this book. You all probably fall into one of three categories. We have some readers who start in the Reclaiming Honor series and have never read my other books or Michael's other books. We have the readers who read ALL my other books, and then came here. And we have Michael's readers who have read his and given me a shot. All are equally amazing, but all come with, I think, wildly different expectations.

I look forward to hearing from you all what you think!

❖ ❖ ❖

If you loved the book, please leave a review and spread the word. ;-)

❖ ❖ ❖

Read the next book, read all of my other books (and Michael's), and join us in this quest to defeat the evil monster that tries to kill discoverability.

If this wasn't your thing? Well... I apologize. All I can say is, hey, both Michael's books and my other books have different feels, so don't give up on us, go read those and see what you think.

With all of this, and the other amazing authors like T.S. Paul and Craig Martelle writing in Michael's Kurtherian universe, you have options. You should have plenty to read, and plenty to fall in love with.

Looking to take a chance on my other books? YAY! You make me so happy. Here's a bit about some of the series I have and why you might enjoy them.

❖ ❖ ❖

FALLS OF REDEMPTION
amzn.to/2kpjFaM

I think you'll like this fantasy series because I start out very NOT fantasy. It's regular people and their problems, in a made up world loosely based on Ancient Greece and the Peloponnesian War. But there are hints of the 'magic' to come. No extra races or crazy magicians - this is fantasy for people who want something more grounded... until the shifter dragon stuff starts happening, haha.

❖ ❖ ❖

THE CURSED NIGHT
amzn.to/2l0Xk5w

This series, starting with Hounds of God, should be right up your alley. It's about a woman dealing with being a werewolf and trying to find a cure, while a half-vampire hunts her down as part of his quest to rid the world of werewolves. It gets more complicated as full vampires show up and an army of werewolves infiltrates the military, but yeah, you get the picture. Superhero werewolf and vampire stuff. Who doesn't love that?

❖ ❖ ❖

ALLIE STROM: THE BRINGER OF LIGHT TRILOGY
amzn.to/2kk9p8u

Want something a bit lighter and for a YA audience? A lot of adults like to read YA (me included, which is why I write it. Actually, a lot of Harry Potter readers were adults). This one is basically the story of a girl who rises to save the world, using the magic from the ring of Solomon. It goes to Kyrgyzstan and the Throne of Solomon, Japan, and other cool places. Fun Urban Fantasy for a younger audience.

❖ ❖ ❖

MODERN NECROMANCY
amzn.to/2kkgIgB

This series starts with Death Marked. (Sounds pretty dark, right?)

Yeah, it is in some ways, but like all my stories, it is really a superhero coming of age. It starts with a guy who wants to talk with his deceased fiancé one more time, maybe even bring her back, but quickly 180s into a story of him trying to stop a mad-man from raising an army of the dead.

Oh yeah, and the hero has to partner up with a badass female ghost. This is another one of those books for aspiring travelers, as it goes to Uzbekistan, Russia, Peru, and more (throughout the trilogy - not all at once). If you want to see a man and woman team up to defeat evil forces, this is the series. Wait, that's all of my series! But this one fits in there well with the rest, in a very unique way.

And then there are all of my books for children, including some unofficial Minecraft ones. I don't want to go on and on, so I'll leave it at that and say that I hope you check out the books! Cross-discoverability is the life-blood of an author. At least, this author. You can find them on my Amazon page (amzn.to/2lCFoBb).

Thank you for reading, and stay tuned for book 4!

Justin Sloan

AUTHOR'S NOTES - MICHAEL ANDERLE

Written: Feruary 14, 2017

Right now, as I type this, it is 12:05 PM on Valentines day and this book is about to be released in just a few, short, hours.

"OMG - HOW DID HE GET AWAY WITH THIS?"

(What? You mean how did I get away with working on Valentines Day? I treated my wife to a LOOONG night out Sunday night, she flew home, now she is comotose in bed… I'm good until she wakes back up and by that time, I'll have hit 'published' on this book. See, crises averted!)

For those who have read my Author's Notes in the back of It's Hell To Choose (The Kurtherian Gambit #09), you might remember me telling a story how I was 'weeping' at the death of a character…I'm talking TEARS streaming down my face as I wrote a scene.

Was the Author's Wife, when hearing of The Author's manly display of emotions after he published the book, supportive?

Not even close.

She laughed her ass off. Moreover, she remembered a Snoopy scene (supposedly) where Snoopy is sitting on top of his doghouse, typing a book and crying his eyes out…

She would walk around our bedroom, mime typing in the air and throw her head back, crying "WAAAHH wah wah wah!"

Then, she would kill herself laughing again.

The Author's feelings were obviously not high on her priority list.

I say this because I am typing this Author's note and looking at a big white coffee mug, with Snoopy on the side, two red hearts and a Snoopy Plush doll sitting inside of it.

Perhaps this is her apology for that reaction half a year ago?

Yeah, I'm not getting my hopes up, either. It is, however, part of the history of our relationship and the part that I love about her. She is fun, exciting and occasionally ignorant of the travails of a writer.

Oh well, such is life.

A lot has happened since the last book in the Reclaiming Honor series. We (The Kurtherian Gambit Series of Books) are playfully kicking each other out of spots in various category charts.

Poor Craig Martelle (The Terry Henry Walton Chronicles - now to be known as "Awesome Craig") keeps putting his books out at the wrong time. and so his series gets *book blocked* from being a Bestseller by either my book, or Justin's book. When he could have taken over the Vampire subcategory last month, he couldn't JOIN the category because he didn't have a vampire in his story, and someone else had a really strong Werewolf story when Justin dropped out of #1.

Now, his latest (Nomad Unleashed) dropped just three days after a new Bethany Anne story (Never Submit) and let's face it, trying to compete with *the* character that started all of this is never a good idea.

So, he has stayed in 2nd place behind my book. Now, Justin's book will probably kick my book out of first place. I'll go to #2, and Craig will go to #3.

Interestingly enough, I'll actually be in all three ;-)

Fortunately, CM Raymond's and Lee Barbant's story will be in another category, so we don't have to fight with them.

However, Holly *Freaking* Dodd is going to be in PNR, so theoretically we might have to compete with her, and ROMANCE readers are damned voracious!

We might all have to bow at the sales altar of Romance and the boys will all have to pick up our toys and play in Space Marines or something!

That assumes that Natalie Grey doesn't kick us out… DAMN!

The next Valerie story is titled "Angel of Reckoning" - Valerie will be coming back at you in April, 2017.

If you want to see more about the other series, the links are below…as well as a picture of my Valentine's Day gift!

Michael

❖ ❖ ❖

The Kurtherian Gambit
Starting with Death Becomes Her

https://www.amazon.com/Death-Becomes-Kurtherian-Gambit-Book-ebook/dp/B017I3NVP2

This is the "master" series, the one that started it all.
What you thought you knew about Vampires and Weres is Wrong … So very, very wrong.

❖ ❖ ❖

The Boris Chronicles
Starting with Evacuation

https://www.amazon.com/Evacuation-Boris-Chronicles-Book-1-ebook/dp/B01IH4V6V2

The first of the series connected with The Kurtherian

Gambit. Boris is a mercenary with a deep past, and a burning desire to protect those in the deepest of Mother Russia.

❖ ❖ ❖

The Terry Henry Walton Chronicles
Starting with Nomad Found
https://www.amazon.com/gp/product/B01N4G6YA3

They say behind every great man is a great woman, but what if that woman is a Werewolf?

❖ ❖ ❖

Etheric Academy
Starting with Alpha Class
https://www.amazon.com/Alpha-Class-Kurtherian-Etheric-Academy-ebook/dp/B01N9NRGB5

Our YA series readers can enjoy, and share with the younger crowd without worrying about the language nearly as much! Following some of our younger (teen) students as they learn more about what it will take to support the Etheric Empire.

❖ ❖ ❖

Keep on the lookout, more series coming soon ;-)

JUSTIN SLOAN SOCIAL

For a chance to see ALL of Justin's different Book Series Check out his website below!

Website:
http://JustinSloanAuthor.com

Email List:
http://JustinSloanAuthor.com/Newsletter

Facebook Here:
https://www.facebook.com/JustinSloanAuthor

MICHAEL ANDERLE SOCIAL

Website:
http://kurtherianbooks.com/

Email List:
http://kurtherianbooks.com/email-list/

Facebook Here:
https://www.facebook.com/TheKurtherianGambitBooks/

STORIES BY JUSTIN SLOAN

CURSED NIGHT

Hounds of God

FALLS OF REDEMPTION (TRILOGY)

Land of Gods
Retribution Calls
Tears of Devotion

RECLAIMING HONOR (A KURTHERIAN GAMBIT SERIES)

Justice is Calling (Audiobook available)
Claimed By Honor (Audiobook coming soon)
Judgment Has Fallen (Audiobook coming)
Angel of Reckoning (April 2017)

MODERN NECROMANCY (TRILOGY)

Death Marked
Death Bound
Death Crowned

ALLIE STROM (TRILOGY)

Allie Strom and the Ring of Solomon
Allie Strom and the Sword of the Spirit
Allie Strom and the Tenth Worthy

STORIES BY MICHAEL ANDERLE

KURTHERIN GAMBIT SERIES TITLES INCLUDE:

FIRST ARC

Death Becomes Her (01) - Queen Bitch (02) - Love Lost (03) - Bite This (04) - Never Forsaken (05) - Under My Heel (06) - Kneel Or Die (07)

SECOND ARC

We Will Build (08) - It's Hell To Choose (09) - Release The Dogs of War (10) - Sued For Peace (11) - We Have Contact (12) - My Ride is a Bitch (13) - Don't Cross This Line (14)

THIRD ARC *(Due 2017)*

Never Submit (15) - Never Surrender (16) - Forever Defend (17) - Might Makes Right (18) - Ahead Full (19) - Capture Death (20) - Life Goes On (21)

New Series

THE SECOND DARK AGES
(Michael's Return)

The Dark Messiah
The Darkest Night (04.2017)
Darkest Before the Dawn (07.2017)
Light Is Breaking (11.2017)

THE BORIS CHRONICLES
With Paul C. Middleton

Evacuation
Retaliation
Revelation
Restitution (*2017*)

RECLAIMING HONOR
With Justin Sloan

Justice Is Calling (01)
Claimed By Honor (02)
Judgment Has Fallen (03)

THE ETHERIC ACADEMY
With TS Paul

ALPHA CLASS (01)
ALPHA CLASS (02) (*02/03 2017*)
ALPHA CLASS (03) (*05/06 2017*)

TERRY HENRY "TH" WALTON CHRONICLES
With Craig Martelle

Nomad Found
Nomad Redeemed
Nomad Unleashed (02/03 2017)

SHORT STORIES

Frank Kurns Stories of the Unknownworld 01 (*7.5*)
You Don't Mess with John's Cousin

Frank Kurns Stories of the Unknownworld 02 (*9.5*)
Bitch's Night Out

Frank Kurns Stories of the Unknownworld 03 (13.25)
With Natalie Grey
BELLATRIX

AUDIOBOOKS
Available at Audible.com and iTunes

The Kurtherian Gambit

Death Becomes Her - Available Now
Queen Bitch – Coming Soon
Love Lost – Coming Soon

Reclaiming Honor Series

Justice Is Calling – Available Now
Claimed By Honor – Coming Soon
Judgement Has Fallen - Coming Soon

ANTHOLOGIES

Glimpse
Honor in Death
(Michael's First Few Days)

Beyond the Stars: At Galaxy's Edge
Tabitha's Vacation

Made in the USA
Lexington, KY
19 July 2017